THE KINGFISHER BOOK OF

Great BOY Stories

*For all my grandchildren,
boys and girls—M. M.*

ISBN 0-439-45303-8

THE KINGFISHER BOOK OF
Great
BOY
Stories

A TREASURY OF CLASSICS FROM CHILDREN'S LITERATURE

Chosen by Michael Morpurgo

SCHOLASTIC INC.
New York Toronto London Auckland Sydney
Mexico City New Delhi Hong Kong Buenos Aires

CONTENTS

FOREWORD

"Lights out!" And the halls were plunged into sudden blackness. I was left alone with my thoughts—thoughts of tomorrow, of the trouble I'd be in; thoughts of home and happier places, happier times. I always dreaded "lights out," dreaded the loneliness of the dark. But in time I found the comfort I needed. I found it in a book, in reading.

I had a flashlight. I had a book. I would burrow backward down my bed and cocoon myself in the secret glow of the flashlight, open my book, and then lose myself in the story. I could go over the seas to treasure islands, or I could live in haunted houses, in fancy palaces, below decks on a ship. This became my treasured time, a time I loved, a time of thrilling adventure, of suspense, of fantasy, and fun. . . .

I went away to boarding school when I was seven. I had always had books around the house at home, but it was at school that I first discovered a real love of stories. They provided my only real privacy; an escape from the dreary routines of English boarding school—math, semolina, squeaky beds, and the smells of cabbage and shoe polish.

Most of the books I read then were boys' books—about pirates, or pranks, or great heroics. I chose boys' books, I think, because I needed to feel that I was the hero in the book. I found it easier if the hero was a boy or a man. I could put myself in his place, do what he did, go where he went, feel what he felt.

Later on I had a spell when I hardly read at all. Perhaps I could not find the books I liked, or maybe I was busy with other things—busy growing up, being a father, being a teacher. It was as a teacher that I found myself telling my own stories, and then one day I began writing them down. I haven't stopped since. Now

I'm the name on the spine of a book—I still can't quite believe it. I just hope that somewhere, in bed, under the covers, in the secret glow of a flashlight, there's someone reading one of my stories, and loving it, not wanting it to end.

I know now that there's more to a great story than merely the excitement it brings. A great story takes you by the hand, and leads you into new worlds, where you meet new people, where you can live with them through their joys and sorrows. In doing this you discover more about the world, how it is, how it was, how it might be in the future; about why people behave as they do and about your own place in the scheme of things. Every book is a voyage of discovery, of self-discovery, and—best of all—you do the discovering. The writer may write it. But you make the pictures in your head. You see the place, hear the voice. You're inside the story, part of it, in some strange way making it happen. It's genuinely interactive. That's why it works.

All I've tried to do in this book is gather together pieces from some of the stories I've read and loved as a boy—and as a grown-up boy—in the hope that you'll love them, too. From *Winnie-the-Pooh* to *Dragon Slayer*, from *The Jungle Book* to *Treasure Island*, from *Pinocchio* to *Charlie and the Chocolate Factory*—there's something here for everyone. Have a taste of each story—there's not room in this book for more than just a taste. If you like it, find the book in the library, in a bookstore, and then settle down somewhere quiet where you won't be disturbed. I suggest in bed, under the covers, in the secret glow of a flashlight. There's nothing like it!

Michael Morpurgo
Devon, June 2000

Introduction

Winnie-the-Pooh is Christopher Robin's teddy bear.
Pooh (who likes honey—a lot) has friends named
Eeyore, Piglet, and Tigger, and must be just about
the most famous bear the world has ever known.
No other bear gets himself stuck as often as Pooh—
if he isn't getting his head stuck in a pot of honey,
then he's getting himself stuck down a
rabbit hole. "Silly old bear!"

WINNIE~THE~POOH

A. A. MILNE

In Which Pooh Goes Visiting and Gets Into a Tight Place

Edward Bear, known to his friends as Winnie-the-Pooh, or Pooh for short, was walking through the forest one day, humming proudly to himself. He had made up a little hum that very morning, as he was doing his Stoutness Exercises in front of the glass: *Tra-la-la, tra-la-la*, as he stretched up as high as he could go, and then *Tra-la-la, tra-la—oh, help!—la*, as he tried to reach his toes. After breakfast he had said it over and over to himself until he had learnt it off by heart, and now he was humming it right through, properly. It went like this:

> *Tra-la-la, tra-la-la,*
> *Tra-la-la, tra-la-la,*
> *Rum-tum-tiddle-um-tum.*
> *Tiddle-iddle, tiddle-iddle,*
> *Tiddle-iddle, tiddle-iddle,*
> *Rum-tum-tum-tiddle-um.*

Well, he was humming this hum to himself, and walking along gaily, wondering what everybody else was doing, and what it felt like, being somebody else, when suddenly he came to a sandy bank, and in the bank was a large hole.

"Aha!" said Pooh. *(Rum-tum-tiddle-um-tum.)* "If I know anything about anything, that hole means Rabbit," he said, "and Rabbit means Company," he said, "and Company means Food and Listening-to-Me-Humming and such like. *Rum-tum-tum-tiddle-um.*"

So he bent down, put his head into the hole, and called out: "Is anybody at home?"

There was a sudden scuffling noise from inside the hole, and then silence.

"What I said was, 'Is anybody at home?'" called out Pooh very loudly.

"No!" said a voice; and then added, "You needn't shout so loud. I heard you quite well the first time."

"Bother!" said Pooh. "Isn't there anybody here at all?"

"Nobody."

Winnie-the-Pooh took his head out of the hole, and thought for a little, and he thought to himself, "There must be somebody there, because somebody must have *said* 'Nobody.'" So he put his head back in the hole, and said:

"Hallo, Rabbit, isn't that you?"

"No," said Rabbit, in a different sort of voice this time.

"But isn't that Rabbit's voice?"

"I don't *think* so," said Rabbit. "It isn't *meant* to be."

"Oh!" said Pooh.

He took his head out of the hole, and had another think, and then he put it back, and said:

"Well, could you very kindly tell me where Rabbit is?"

"He has gone to see his friend Pooh Bear, who is a great friend of his."

"But this *is* Me!" said Bear, very much surprised.

"What sort of Me?"

"Pooh Bear."

"Are you sure?" said Rabbit, still more surprised.

"Quite, quite sure," said Pooh.

"Oh, well, then, come in."

So Pooh pushed and pushed and pushed his way through the hole, and at last he got in.

"You were quite right," said Rabbit, looking at him all over. "It *is* you. Glad to see you."

"Who did you think it was?"

"Well, I wasn't sure. You know how it is in the Forest. One can't have *anybody* coming into one's house. One has to be *careful*. What about a mouthful of something?"

Pooh always liked a little something at eleven o'clock in the morning, and he was very glad to see Rabbit getting out the plates and mugs; and when Rabbit said, "Honey or condensed milk with your bread?" he was so excited that he said, "Both," and then, so as not to seem greedy, he added, "but don't bother about the bread, please." And for a long time after that he said nothing . . . until at last, humming to himself in a rather sticky voice, he got up, shook Rabbit lovingly by the paw, and said that he must be going on.

"Must you?" said Rabbit politely.

"Well," said Pooh, "I could stay a little longer if it—if you—" and he tried very hard to look in the direction of the larder.

"As a matter of fact," said Rabbit, "I was going out myself directly."

"Oh well, then, I'll be going on. Good-bye."

"Well, good-bye, if you're sure you won't have any more."

"*Is* there any more?" asked Pooh quickly.

Rabbit took the covers off the dishes, and said, no, there wasn't.

"I thought not," said Pooh, nodding to himself. "Well, good-bye. I must be going on."

So he started to climb out of the hole. He pulled with his front paws, and pushed with his back paws, and in a little while his nose was out in the open again . . . and then his ears . . . and then his front paws . . . and then his shoulders . . . and then—

"Oh, help!" said Pooh. "I'd better go back."

"Oh, bother!" said Pooh. "I shall have to go on."

"I can't do either!" said Pooh. "Oh, help *and* bother!"

Now by this time Rabbit wanted to go for a walk too, and finding the front door full, he went out by the back door, and came round to Pooh, and looked at him.

"Hallo, are you stuck?" he asked.

"N-no," said Pooh carelessly. "Just resting and thinking and humming to myself."

"Here, give us a paw."

Pooh Bear stretched out a paw, and Rabbit pulled and pulled and pulled. . . .

"*Ow!*" cried Pooh. "You're hurting!"

"The fact is," said Rabbit, "you're stuck."

"It all comes," said Pooh crossly, "of not having front doors big enough."

"It all comes," said Rabbit sternly, "of eating too much. I thought at the time," said Rabbit, "only I didn't like to say anything," said Rabbit, "that one of us was eating too much," said Rabbit, "and I knew it wasn't *me,*" he said. "Well, well, I shall go and fetch Christopher Robin."

Christopher Robin lived at the other end of the Forest, and when he came back with Rabbit, and saw the front half of Pooh, he said, "Silly old Bear," in such a loving voice that everybody felt quite hopeful again.

"I was just beginning to think," said Bear, sniffing slightly, "that Rabbit might never be able to use his front door again. And I should *hate* that," he said.

"So should I," said Rabbit.

"Use his front door again?" said Christopher Robin. "Of course he'll use his front door again."

"Good," said Rabbit.

"If we can't pull you out, Pooh, we might push you back."

Rabbit scratched his whiskers thoughtfully, and pointed out that, when once Pooh was pushed back, he was back, and of course nobody was more glad to see Pooh than *he* was, still there it was, some lived in trees and some lived underground, and—

"You mean I'd *never* get out?" said Pooh.

"I mean," said Rabbit, "that having got *so* far, it seems a pity to waste it."

Christopher Robin nodded.

"Then there's only one thing to be done," he said. "We shall have to wait for you to get thin again."

"How long does getting thin take?" asked Pooh anxiously.

"About a week, I should think."

"But I can't stay here for a *week*!"

"You can *stay* here all right, silly old Bear. It's getting you out which is so difficult."

"We'll read to you," said Rabbit cheerfully. "And I hope it won't snow," he added. "And I say, old fellow, you're taking up a good deal of room in my house—*do* you mind if I use your back legs as a towel-horse? Because, I mean, there they are—doing nothing—and it would be very convenient just to hang the towels on them."

"A week!" said Pooh gloomily. *"What about meals?"*

"I'm afraid no meals," said Christopher Robin, "because of getting thin quicker. But we *will* read to you."

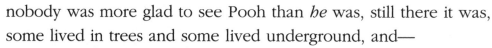

Bear began to sigh, and then found he couldn't because he was so tightly stuck; and a tear rolled down his eye, as he said:

"Then would you read a Sustaining Book, such as would help and comfort a Wedged Bear in Great Tightness?"

So for a week Christopher Robin read that sort of book

at the North end of Pooh, and
Rabbit hung his washing on the
South end . . . and in between
Bear felt himself getting
slenderer and slenderer.
And at the end of the
week Christopher Robin
said, *"Now!"*

So he took hold of Pooh's
front paws and Rabbit took hold
of Christopher Robin, and all Rabbit's friends and relations took
hold of Rabbit, and they all pulled together. . . .

And for a long time Pooh only said *"Ow!"* . . .

And *"Oh!"* . . .

And then, all of a sudden, he said *"Pop!"* just as if a cork were
coming out of a bottle.

And Christopher Robin and Rabbit and all Rabbit's friends and
relations went head-over-heels backwards . . . and on top of them
came Winnie-the-Pooh—free!

So, with a nod of thanks to his friends, he went on with
his walk through the Forest, humming proudly to himself. But,
Christopher Robin looked after him lovingly, and said to himself,
"Silly old Bear!"

Introduction

If you pick up a copy of Flat Stanley, *you'll find
it's fairly flat (not a lot of pages, but an awful lot
of fun), just like Stanley Lambchop himself. It's not
Stanley's fault that he has been squashed flat by an
enormous bulletin board falling on his bed! Some
people might think it's a disadvantage to be
completely flat—not Stanley. Once he gets used
to it, he really enjoys it: Stanley can be a kite
when he feels like it; he can get himself mailed in
an envelope to his friends in California; he can
even be framed as a painting on a wall.
And that comes in handy, as you'll see.*

F LAT S TANLEY

JEFF BROWN

Mr. and Mrs. O. Jay Dart lived in the apartment above the Lambchops. Mr. Dart was an important man, the director of the Famous Museum of Art downtown in the city.

Stanley Lambchop had noticed in the elevator that Mr. Dart, who was ordinarily a cheerful man, had become quite gloomy, but he had no idea what the reason was. And then at breakfast one morning he heard Mr. and Mrs. Lambchop talking about Mr. Dart.

"I see," said Mr. Lambchop, reading the paper over his coffee cup, "that still another painting has been stolen from the Famous Museum. It says here that Mr. O. Jay Dart, the director, is at his wits' end."

"Oh, dear! Are the police no help?" Mrs. Lambchop asked.

"It seems not," said Mr. Lambchop. "Listen to what the Chief of Police told the newspaper. 'We suspect a gang of sneak thieves. These are the worst kind. They work by sneakery, which makes them very difficult to catch. However, my men and I will keep trying. Meanwhile, I hope people will buy tickets for the Policemen's Ball and not park their cars where signs say don't.'"

The next morning Stanley Lambchop heard Mr. Dart talking to his wife in the elevator.

"These sneak thieves work at night," Mr. Dart said. "It is very hard for our guards to stay awake when they have been on duty all day. And the Famous Museum is so big, we cannot guard every picture at the same time. I fear it is hopeless, hopeless, hopeless!"

Suddenly, as if an electric light bulb had lit up in the air above his head, giving out little shooting lines of excitement, Stanley Lambchop had an idea. He told it to Mr. Dart.

"Stanley," Mr. Dart said, "if your mother will give her permission, I will put you and your plan to work this very night!"

Mrs. Lambchop gave her permission. "But you will have to take a long nap this afternoon," she said. "I won't have you up till all hours unless you do."

That evening, after a long nap, Stanley went with Mr. Dart to the Famous Museum. Mr. Dart took him into the main hall, where the biggest and most important paintings were hung. He pointed to a huge painting that showed a bearded man, wearing a floppy velvet hat, playing a violin for a lady who lay on a couch. There was a half-man, half-horse person standing behind them, and three fat children with wings were flying around above. That, Mr. Dart explained, was the most expensive painting in the world!

There was an empty picture frame on the opposite wall. We shall hear more about that later on.

Mr. Dart took Stanley into his office and said, "It is time for you to put on a disguise."

"I already thought of that," Stanley Lambchop said, "and I brought one. My cowboy suit. It has a red bandanna that I can tie over my face. Nobody will recognize me in a million years."

"No," Mr. Dart said. "You will have to wear the disguise I have chosen."

From a closet he took a white dress with a blue sash, a pair of shiny little pointed shoes, a wide straw hat with a blue band that matched the sash, and a wig and a stick. The wig was made of

blond hair, long and done in ringlets. The stick was curved at the top and it, too, had a blue ribbon on it.

"In this shepherdess disguise," Mr. Dart said, "you will look like a painting that belongs in the main hall. We do not have cowboy pictures in the main hall."

Stanley was so disgusted, he could hardly speak. "I will look like a girl, that's what I will look like," he said. "I wish I had never had my idea."

But he was a good sport, so he put on the disguise.

Back in the main hall, Mr. Dart helped Stanley climb up into the empty picture frame. Stanley was able to stay in place because Mr. Dart had cleverly put four small spikes in the wall, one for each hand and foot.

The frame was a perfect fit. Against the wall, Stanley looked just like a picture.

"Except for one thing," Mr. Dart said. "Shepherdesses are supposed to look happy. They smile at their sheep and at the sky. You look fierce, not happy, Stanley."

Stanley tried hard to get a faraway look in his eyes and even to smile a little bit.

Mr. Dart stood back a few feet and stared at him for a moment. "Well," he said, "it may not be art, but I know what I like."

He went off to make sure that certain other parts of Stanley's plan were taken care of, and Stanley was left alone.

It was very dark in the main hall. A little bit of moonlight came through the windows, and Stanley could just make out the world's most expensive painting on the opposite wall. He felt as though the bearded man with the violin and the lady on the couch and the half-horse person and the winged children were all waiting, as he was, for something to happen.

Time passed and he got tireder and tireder. Anyone would be tired this late at night, especially if he had to stand in a picture frame balancing on little spikes.

Maybe they won't come, Stanley thought. Maybe the sneak thieves won't come at all.

The moon went behind a cloud and then the main hall was pitch-dark. It seemed to get quieter, too, with the darkness. There was absolutely no sound at all. Stanley felt the hair on the back of his neck prickle beneath the golden curls of the wig.

Cr-eee-eee-k . . .

The creaking sound came from right out in the middle of the main hall, and even as he heard it, Stanley saw, in the same place, a tiny yellow glow of light!

The creaking came again, and the glow got bigger. A trapdoor had opened in the floor, and two men came up through it into the hall!

Stanley understood everything all at once. These must be the sneak thieves! They had a secret trapdoor entrance into the museum from outside. That was why they had never been caught. And now, tonight, they were back to steal the most expensive painting in the world!

He held very still in his picture frame and listened to the

sneak thieves.

"This is it, Max," said the first one. "This is where we art robbers pull a sensational job whilst the civilized community sleeps."

"Right, Luther," said the other man. "In all this great city, there

is no one to suspect us."

Ha, ha! thought Stanley Lambchop. That's what you think!

The sneak thieves put down their lantern and took the world's most expensive painting off the wall.

"What would we do to anyone who tried to capture us, Max?" the first man asked.

"We would kill him. What else?" his friend replied.

That was enough to frighten Stanley, and he was even more frightened when Luther came over and stared at him.

"This sheep girl," Luther said. "I thought sheep girls were supposed to smile, Max. This one looks scared."

Just in time, Stanley managed to get a faraway look in his eyes again and to smile, sort of.

"You're crazy, Luther," Max said. "She's smiling. And what a pretty little thing she is, too."

That made Stanley furious. He waited until the sneak thieves had turned back to the world's most expensive painting, and he shouted in his loudest, most terrifying voice: "POLICE! POLICE! MR.

DART! THE SNEAK THIEVES ARE HERE!"

The sneak thieves looked at each other. "Max," said the first one, very quietly, "I think I heard the sheep girl yell."

"I think I did too," said Max in a quivery voice. "Oh, boy! Yelling pictures. We both need a rest."

"You'll get a rest, all right!" shouted Mr. Dart, rushing in with the Chief of Police and lots of guards and policemen behind him. "You'll get *ar-rested*, that's what! Ha, ha, ha!"

The sneak thieves were too mixed up by Mr. Dart's joke and too frightened by the policemen to put up a fight.

Before they knew it, they had been handcuffed and led away to jail.

The next morning in the office of the Chief of Police, Stanley Lambchop got a medal. The day after that his picture was in all the newspapers.

For a while Stanley Lambchop was a famous name. Everywhere that Stanley went, people stared and pointed at him. He could hear them whisper, "Over there, Agnes, over there! That must be Stanley Lambchop, the one who caught the sneak thieves . . ." and things like that.

But after a few weeks the whispering and the staring stopped. People had other things to think about. Stanley did not mind. Being famous had been fun, but enough was enough.

Introduction

Mr. and Mrs. Darling have gone out, leaving their three children, John, Michael, and Wendy, safely tucked into bed—or so they think. Nana the dog senses something is wrong up in the nursery. She barks and barks before running off to raise the alarm. But by the time Mr. and Mrs. Darling get home, it's too late. From the street they can see the nursery lights are on, and the children are flying through the air, around and around—and not three children, but four. Peter Pan is taking the children to Neverland. Fly off with them for the greatest adventure of your life.

PETER PAN

J. M. BARRIE

The Flight

"Second to the right, and straight on till morning."

That, Peter had told Wendy, was the way to the Neverland; but even birds, carrying maps and consulting them at windy corners, could not have sighted it with these instructions. Peter, you see, just said anything that came into his head.

At first his companions trusted him implicitly, and so great were the delights of flying that they wasted time circling round church spires or any other tall objects on the way that took their fancy.

John and Michael raced, Michael getting a start.

They recalled with contempt that not so long ago they had thought themselves fine fellows for being able to fly round a room.

Not so long ago. But how long ago? They were flying over the sea before this thought began to disturb Wendy seriously. John thought it was their second sea and their third night.

Sometimes it was dark and sometimes light, and now they were very cold and again too warm. Did they really feel hungry

at times, or were they merely pretending because Peter had such a jolly new way of feeding them? His way was to pursue birds who had food in their mouths suitable for humans and snatch it from them; then the birds would follow and snatch it back; and they would all go chasing each other gaily for miles, parting at last with mutual expressions of good-will. But Wendy noticed with gentle concern that Peter did not seem to know that this was rather an odd way of getting your bread and butter, nor even that there are other ways.

Certainly they did not pretend to be sleepy, they were sleepy; and that was a danger, for the moment they popped off, down they fell. The awful thing was that Peter thought this funny.

"There he goes again!" he would cry gleefully, as Michael suddenly dropped like a stone.

"Save him, save him!" cried Wendy, looking with horror at the cruel sea far below. Eventually Peter would dive through the air, and catch Michael just before he could strike the sea, and it was lovely the way he did it; but he always waited till the last moment, and you felt it was his cleverness that interested him and not the saving of human life. Also he was fond of variety, and the sport that engrossed him one moment would suddenly cease to engage him, so there was always the possibility that the next time you fell he would let you go.

He could sleep in the air without falling, by merely lying on his back and floating, but this was, partly at least, because he was so light that if you got behind him and blew he went faster.

"Do be more polite to him," Wendy whispered to John, when they were playing "Follow my Leader."

"Then tell him to stop showing off," said John.

When playing Follow my Leader, Peter would fly close to the water and touch each shark's tail in passing, just as in the street

you may run your finger along an iron railing. They could not follow him in this with much success, so perhaps it was rather like showing off, especially as he kept looking behind to see how many tails they missed.

"You must be nice to him," Wendy impressed on her brothers. "What would we do if he were to leave us?"

"We could go back," Michael said.

"How could we ever find our way back without him?"

"Well, then, we could go on," said John.

"That is the awful thing, John. We should have to go on, for we don't know how to stop."

This was true; Peter had forgotten to show them how to stop.

John said that if the worst came to the worst, all they had to do was to go straight on, for the world was round, and so in time they must come back to their own window.

"And who is to get food for us, John?"

"I nipped a bit out of that eagle's mouth pretty neatly, Wendy."

"After the twentieth try," Wendy reminded him. "And even though we became good at picking up food, see how we bump against clouds and things if he is not near to give us a hand."

Indeed they were constantly bumping. They could now fly strongly, though they still kicked far too much; but if they saw a cloud in front of them, the more they tried to avoid it, the more certainly did they bump into it. If Nana had been with them she would have had a bandage round Michael's forehead by this time.

Peter was not with them for the moment, and they felt rather lonely up there by themselves. He could go so much faster than they that he would suddenly shoot out of sight, to have some adventure in which they had no share. He would come down laughing over something fearfully funny he had been saying to a star, but he had already forgotten what it was, or he would

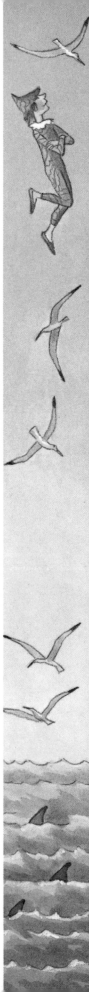

come up with mermaid scales still sticking to him, and yet not be able to say for certain what had been happening. It was really rather irritating to children who had never seen a mermaid.

"And if he forgets them so quickly," Wendy argued, "how can we expect that he will go on remembering us?"

Indeed, sometimes when he returned he did not remember them, at least not well. Wendy was sure of it. She saw recognition come into his eyes as he was about to pass them the time of day and go on; once even she had to tell him her name.

"I'm Wendy," she said agitatedly.

He was very sorry. "I say, Wendy," he whispered to her, "always if you see me forgetting you, just keep on saying 'I'm Wendy,' and then I'll remember."

Of course this was rather unsatisfactory. However, to make amends he showed them how to lie out flat on a strong wind that was going their way, and this was such a pleasant change that they tried it several times and found they could sleep thus with security. Indeed they would have slept longer, but Peter tired quickly of sleeping, and soon he would cry in his captain voice, "We get off here." So with occasional tiffs, but on the whole rollicking, they drew near the Neverland; for after many moons they did reach it, and, what is more, they had been going pretty straight all the time, not perhaps so much owing to the guidance of Peter or Tink as because the island was out looking for them. It is only thus that anyone may sight those magic shores.

"There it is," said Peter calmly.

"Where, where?"

"Where all the arrows are pointing."

Indeed a million golden arrows were pointing out the island to the children, all directed by their friend the sun, who wanted them to be sure of their way before leaving them for the night.

Wendy and John and Michael stood on tiptoe in the air to get their first sight of the island. Strange to say, they all recognized it at once, and until fear fell upon them they hailed it, not as something long dreamt of and seen at last, but as a familiar friend to whom they were returning home for the holidays.

"John, there's the lagoon."

"Wendy, look at the turtles burying their eggs in the sand."

"I say, John, I see your flamingo with the broken leg."

"Look, Michael, there's your cave."

"John, what's that in the brushwood?"

"It's a wolf with her whelps. Wendy, I do believe that's your little whelp."

"There's my boat, John, with her sides stove in."

"No, it isn't. Why, we burned your boat."

"That's her, at any rate. I say, John, I see the smoke of the redskin camp."

"Where? Show me, and I'll tell you by the way the smoke curls whether they are on the war-path."

"There, just across the Mysterious River."

"I see now. Yes, they are on the war-path right enough."

Peter was a little annoyed with them for knowing so much; but if he wanted to lord it over them his triumph was at hand, for have I not told you that anon fear fell upon them?

It came as the arrows went, leaving the island in gloom.

In the old days at home the Neverland had always begun to look a little dark and threatening by bedtime. Then unexplored patches arose in it and spread; black shadows moved about in them; the roar of the beasts of prey was quite different now, and above all, you lost the certainty that you would win. You were quite glad that the night-lights were on. You even liked Nana to say that this was just the mantelpiece over here, and that the

Neverland was all make-believe.

Of course the Neverland had been make-believe in those days; but it was real now, and there were no night-lights, and it was getting darker every moment, and where was Nana?

They had been flying apart, but they huddled close to Peter now. His careless manner had gone at last, his eyes were sparkling, a tingle went through them every time they touched his body. They were now over the fearsome island, flying so low that sometimes a tree grazed their face. Nothing horrid was visible in the air, yet their progress had become slow and labored, exactly as if they were pushing their way through hostile forces. Sometimes they hung in the air until Peter had beaten on it with his fists.

"They don't want us to land," he explained.

"Who are they?" Wendy whispered, shuddering.

But he could not or would not say. Tinker Bell had been asleep on his shoulder, but now he wakened her and sent her on in front.

Sometimes he poised himself in the air, listening intently with his hand to his ear, and again he would stare down with eyes so bright that they seemed to bore two holes to earth. Having done these things, he went on again.

His courage was almost appalling. "Do you want an adventure now," he said casually to John, "or would you like to have your tea first?"

Introduction

Geppetto, the old village woodcarver, wants
to make a puppet—a boy puppet. But he gets
more than he bargained for. He makes it so
well that his puppet becomes a virtual boy.
Geppetto soon finds out that his Pinocchio,
just like most boys, has a mind of
his own. And like any other boy, he gets
himself into all kinds of trouble. Luckily he
meets a good fairy, who often helps him out.
In this excerpt, Pinocchio is saying and doing
anything he can to avoid taking his medicine.
When I was a boy, I used to raise a fuss about
taking my medicine—I still do—but I was
an angel compared to Pinocchio!

PINOCCHIO

CARLO COLLODI

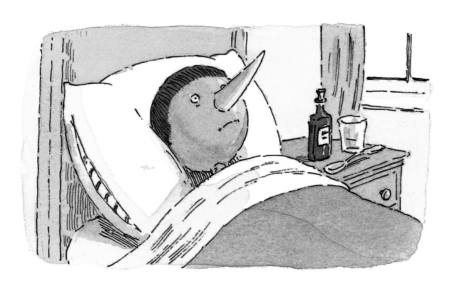

As soon as the three doctors had left the room, the fairy came to Pinocchio. She touched his forehead with her hand, and felt that he had a dangerous fever.

Thereupon she dissolved some white powder in half a glass of water and, holding it to his lips, said lovingly, "Drink this, and in a few days you will be better."

Pinocchio looked at the glass, made a sour face, and asked in a complaining voice, "Is it sweet, or bitter?"

"It is bitter, but it will do you good."

"If it's bitter I won't drink it."

"Listen to me, and drink it!"

"I don't like anything bitter."

"If you drink it, I shall give you a lump of sugar, to take the taste out of your mouth."

"Where is the lump of sugar?"

"Here it is," said the fairy, taking one out of a golden sugar basin.

"First I want the lump of sugar, and then I'll drink the horrid bitter water."

"You promise to drink it?"

"Yes."

The fairy gave him the sugar, and Pinocchio crunched and swallowed it in a second, saying as he licked his lips, "It would be fine if sugar were medicine. I'd take it every day."

"Now keep your promise, and drink these few drops of water. They will bring back your health."

Pinocchio took the glass in his hand unwillingly. He brought it to his nose, and held it to his lips, then again to his nose, and at last he said, "It's too bitter! It's too bitter! I can't drink it."

"How can you tell, when you haven't even tasted it!"

"Oh, I know it is! I know from its smell. Give me another lump of sugar, and then I'll drink it."

So the fairy, with all the patience of a good mother, put another lump of sugar in his mouth, and then she offered him the glass again.

"I can't drink it like that," said the puppet, making hundreds of grimaces.

"Why can't you?"

"Because that pillow on my feet annoys me."

The fairy removed the pillow.

"It's no use. I can't drink it like that, either."

"What is the matter now?"

"The door bothers me; it's half open."

The fairy went and shut the door.

"The fact is," cried Pinocchio, bursting into tears, "I won't drink that bitter water—no, no, no. . . ."

"My child, you will be sorry."

"I don't care."

"You are very ill."

"I don't care."

"This fever will send you to the other world in a few hours."

"I don't care."

"Are you not afraid to die?"

"Not a bit! I'd rather die than drink that horrid medicine!"

At that moment the door of the room opened, and four rabbits as black as ink came in, carrying a little black coffin on their shoulders.

"What do you want of me?" shouted Pinocchio, sitting up in his bed in terror.

"We have come to take you away," said the biggest rabbit.

"To take me away! But I'm not dead yet!"

"No, not quite yet, but you have only a few minutes to live, because you refused the medicine that would have made you well."

"O fairy, kind fairy," cried the puppet, "give me the glass at once; hurry, for Heaven's sake, for I don't want to die! No, I will not die!"

He took the glass in both hands, and emptied it at a draught.

"Ah, well!" said the rabbits. "This time we have made a journey for nothing." And taking the little coffin on their shoulders they left the room, murmuring and grumbling between their teeth.

A few minutes later Pinocchio jumped out of bed quite well; for you must know that wooden marionettes have the privilege of being ill very seldom and of getting well very quickly.

When the fairy saw him running and rushing about the room as gay and lively as a young rooster, she said, "So my medicine really did you good?"

"I should say so! It brought me back to life."

"Then, for Heaven's sake, why was it so hard to make you drink it?"

"I think because we boys are all like that. We fear the medicine more than the sickness."

"Shame on you! Boys should know that the right medicine, taken in time, might save them from a serious illness, perhaps even from death."

"Oh, another time I won't make so much fuss. I'll remember those black rabbits with the coffin on their shoulders, and take the glass at once, and down it will go!"

"Now, come here, and tell me how it happened that you fell into the hands of assassins."

"It was like this: the Showman, Fire-eater, gave me some gold pieces and said, 'Here, take these to your father.' But on the road I met the fox and the cat, two very decent people, and they said, 'Would you like to change these pieces into a thousand—yes, into two thousand—gold pieces? Come with us, and we will take you to the Field of Miracles.' So I said, 'Let us go!' And they said, 'Let's stop at the Red Crab Inn, and continue our way after midnight.' And when I woke up they were not there, because they had left already. Then I started after them in the dark, and I couldn't tell you how dark it was. And so I met two assassins in coal sacks, who said to me, 'Hand over your money!' And I said, 'I haven't any,' because I had hidden the four gold pieces in my mouth. One of the assassins tried to put his hand in my mouth, and I bit it off; but what I spat out wasn't a hand, but a cat's paw. And the assassins ran after me, and I ran and ran until they caught me, and hung me by the neck to a tree in the wood, saying, 'We'll come back tomorrow, and then you will be dead, and your mouth will be open, and we'll get the money hidden under your tongue.'"

"Where are the four gold pieces now?" asked the fairy.

"I've lost them," answered Pinocchio. But he told a lie, for he had them in his pocket. No sooner had he told this lie than his nose, which was already very long, became two inches longer.

"Where did you lose them?"

"In the wood near by."

At this second lie, his nose became still longer.

"If you lost them near here," said the fairy, "we can search for them; for everything lost in that wood can easily be found."

"Oh! Now I remember everything," replied the puppet, greatly confused. "I didn't lose the money. I swallowed it when I was drinking your medicine."

At this third lie, his nose grew so long that poor Pinocchio could not move in any direction. If he turned one way, his nose hit the bed or the window panes; if he turned the other, it struck the walls or the door; if he raised his head a little, there was danger of putting his nose into the fairy's eyes.

The fairy looked at him, and laughed.

"What are you laughing at?" asked the puppet, much

embarrassed and worried about his nose, which was growing to such a size.

"I am laughing at the lies you have told."

"How did you know I was telling lies?"

"Lies, my dear boy, can easily be recognized. There are two kinds of them: those with short legs, and those with long noses. Your kind have long noses."

Pinocchio wanted to hide his face for shame. He tried to run out of the room, but he could not, for his nose was so long that he could not go through the door.

Introduction

It is cold, bitter cold. Everything that Charlie Bucket tastes seems to be made of ice, and the wind is like a knife on his cheek. Inside, the Bucket family huddle together for warmth. All they can afford are thin, cabbagey meals three times a day. Every day on his way to school, Charlie passes Willy Wonka's chocolate factory and smells the chocolate on the air, taking deep, swallowing breaths, as though he were trying to eat the smell itself. If only he can get lucky and win one of the five golden tickets—then he will win a tour of the chocolate factory and enough candy and chocolate to last the rest of his life.

Miracles do happen.

CHARLIE AND THE
CHOCOLATE FACTORY

ROALD DAHL

The Miracle

The cruel weather went on and on.

And every day, Charlie Bucket grew thinner and thinner. His face became frighteningly white and pinched. The skin was drawn so tightly over the cheeks that you could see the shapes of the bones underneath. It seemed doubtful whether he could go on much longer like this without becoming dangerously ill.

And now, very calmly, with that curious wisdom that seems to come so often to small children in times of hardship, he began to make little changes here and there in some of the things that he did, so as to save his strength. In the mornings, he left the house ten minutes earlier so that he could walk slowly to school, without ever having to run. He sat quietly in the classroom during recess, resting himself, while the others rushed outdoors and threw snowballs and wrestled in the snow. Everything he did now, he did slowly and carefully, to prevent exhaustion.

Then one afternoon, walking back home with the icy wind in his face (and incidentally feeling hungrier than he had ever felt before), his eye was caught suddenly by a piece of paper that was lying in the gutter, in the snow. The paper was of a greenish color, and there was something vaguely familiar about it. Charlie stepped off the curb and bent down to examine it. Part of it was buried under the snow, but he saw at once what it was.

It was a dollar bill!

Quickly he looked around him.

Had somebody just dropped it?

No—that was impossible because of the way part of it was buried.

Several people went hurrying past him on the sidewalk, their chins sunk deep in the collars of their coats, their feet crunching in the snow. None of them was searching for any money; none of them was taking the slightest notice of the small boy crouching in the gutter.

Then was it *his*, this dollar?

Could he *have* it?

Carefully, Charlie pulled it out from under the snow. It was damp and dirty, but otherwise perfect.

A WHOLE dollar!

He held it tightly between his shivering fingers, gazing down at it. It meant one thing to him at that moment, only *one* thing. It meant FOOD.

Automatically, Charlie turned and began moving toward the nearest shop. It was only ten paces away . . . it was a newspaper and stationery store, the kind that sells almost everything, including candy and cigars . . . and what he would *do*, he whispered quickly to himself . . . he would buy one luscious bar of candy and eat it *all* up, every bit of it, right then and there . . . and the rest of the

money he would take straight back home and give to his mother.

Charlie entered the store and laid the damp dollar bill on the counter.

"One Wonka's Whipple-Scrumptious Fudgemallow Delight," he said, remembering how much he had loved the one he had on his birthday.

The man behind the counter looked fat and well-fed. He had big lips and fat cheeks and a very fat neck. The fat around his neck bulged out all around the top of his collar like a rubber ring. He turned and reached behind him for the candy bar, then he turned back again and handed it to Charlie. Charlie grabbed it and quickly tore off the wrapper and took an enormous bite. Then he took another . . . and another . . . and oh, the joy of being able to cram large pieces of something sweet and solid into one's mouth! The sheer blissful joy of being able to fill one's mouth with rich solid food!

"You look like you wanted that one, sonny," the shopkeeper said pleasantly.

Charlie nodded, his mouth bulging with chocolate.

The shopkeeper put Charlie's change on the counter. "Take it easy," he said. "It'll give you a gut-ache if you swallow it like that without chewing."

Charlie went on wolfing the chocolate. He couldn't stop. And in less than half a minute, the whole thing had disappeared down his throat. He was quite out of breath, but he felt marvelously, extraordinarily happy. He reached out a hand to take the change. Then he paused. His eyes were just above the level of the counter. They were staring at the little silver coins lying there. The coins were all dimes. There were nine of them altogether. Surely it wouldn't matter if he spent just one more. . . .

"I think," he said quietly, "I think . . . I'll have just one more of those candy bars. The same kind as before, please."

"Why not?" the fat shopkeeper said, reaching behind him again and taking another Whipple-Scrumptious Fudgemallow Delight from the shelf. He laid it on the counter.

Charlie picked it up and tore off the wrapper . . . and *suddenly* . . . from underneath the wrapper . . . there came a brilliant flash of gold.

Charlie's heart stood still.

"It's a Golden Ticket!" screamed the shopkeeper, leaping about a foot in the air. "You've got a Golden Ticket! You've found the last Golden Ticket! Hey, what do you know! Come and look at this, everybody! The kid's found Wonka's last Golden Ticket! There it is! It's right there in his hands!"

It seemed as though the shopkeeper might be going to have a fit. "In my shop, too!" he yelled. "He found it right here in my own little shop! Somebody call the newspapers quick and let them

know! Watch out now, sonny! Don't tear it as you unwrap it! That thing's precious!"

In a few seconds, there was a crowd of about twenty people clustering around Charlie, and many more were pushing their way in from the street. Everybody wanted to get a look at the Golden Ticket and at the lucky finder.

"Where is it?" somebody shouted. "Hold it up so all of us can see it!"

"There it is, there!" someone else shouted. "He's holding it in his hands! See the gold shining!"

"How did *he* manage to find it, I'd like to know?" a large boy shouted angrily. "*Twenty* bars a day I've been buying for weeks and weeks!"

"Think of all the free stuff he'll be getting too!" another boy said enviously. "A lifetime supply!"

"He'll need it, the skinny little shrimp!" a girl said, laughing.

Charlie hadn't moved. He hadn't even unwrapped the Golden Ticket from around the candy bar. He was standing very still, holding it tightly with both hands while the crowd pushed and shouted all around him. He felt quite dizzy. There was a peculiar floating sensation coming over him, as though he were floating up in the air like a balloon. His feet didn't seem to be touching the ground at all. He could hear his heart thumping away loudly somewhere in his throat.

At that point, he became aware of a hand resting lightly on his shoulder, and when he looked up, he saw a tall man standing over him. "Listen," the man whispered. "I'll buy it from you. I'll give you fifty dollars. How about it, eh? And I'll give you a new bicycle as well. Okay?"

"Are you *crazy?*" shouted a woman who was standing equally close. "Why, I'd give him *five hundred* dollars for that ticket! You

want to sell that ticket for five hundred dollars, young man?"

"That's *quite* enough of that!" the fat shopkeeper shouted, pushing his way through the crowd and taking Charlie firmly by the arm. "Leave the kid alone, will you! Make way there! Let him out!" And to Charlie, as he led him to the door, he whispered, "Don't you let *anybody* have it! Take it straight home, quickly, before you lose it! Run all the way and don't stop till you get there, you understand?"

Charlie nodded.

"You know something," the fat shopkeeper said, pausing a moment and smiling at Charlie, "I have a feeling you needed a break like this. I'm awfully glad you got it. Good luck to you, sonny."

"Thank you," Charlie said, and off he went, running through the snow as fast as his legs would go. And as he flew past Mr. Willy Wonka's factory, he turned and waved at it and sang out, "I'll be seeing you! I'll be seeing you soon!" And five minutes later he arrived at his own home.

Charlie burst through the front door, shouting, *"Mother! Mother! Mother!"*

Mrs. Bucket was in the old grandparents' room, serving them their evening soup.

"Mother!" yelled Charlie, rushing in on them like a hurricane. "Look! I've got it! Look, Mother, look! The last Golden Ticket! It's mine! I found some money in the street and I bought two candy bars and the second one had the Golden Ticket and there were *crowds* of people all around me wanting to see it and the shopkeeper rescued me and I ran all the way home and here I am! *IT'S THE FIFTH GOLDEN TICKET, MOTHER, AND I'VE FOUND IT!"*

Introduction

An only child, Bertie grows up with his mother and father on a remote farm on the South African veld. He spends all his days safely behind the high compound fence around his yard. From here he can watch the animals as they come to the water hole. One day he sees a lioness and her cub coming down to drink. To his astonishment the cub is white, pure white. Day after day, Bertie waits for them to come again, but they don't. Then comes the dreadful news that the lioness has been shot on the farm. Bertie longs for the orphaned cub to come back. But days pass and there is no sign of him. Bertie has almost given up hope. . . .

THE BUTTERFLY LION

MICHAEL MORPURGO

Bertie and the Lion

One morning a week or so later, Bertie was awakened by a
sudden chorus of urgent neighing. He jumped out of his
bed and ran to the window. A herd of zebras was scattering away
from the water hole chased by a couple of hyenas. Then he saw
more hyenas, three of them, standing stock still, noses pointing,
eyes fixed on the water hole. It was only now that Bertie saw the
lion cub. But this one wasn't white at all. He was covered in mud,
his back to the water hole, and he was waving a pathetic paw
at the hyenas, who were beginning to circle. The lion cub had
nowhere to run to, and the hyenas were sidling ever closer.

Bertie was downstairs in a flash, leaping off the veranda and
racing barefoot across the compound, shouting at the top of his
voice. He threw open the gate and charged down the hill toward
the water hole, yelling and screaming and waving his arms like a
wild thing. Startled at this sudden intrusion, the hyenas turned tail
and ran, but not far. Once within range Bertie hurled a broadside
of pebbles at them, and they ran off again, but again not far.

Then he was at the water hole and between the lion cub and the hyenas, shouting at them to go away. They didn't. They stood and watched, uncertain for a while. Then they began to circle again, closer, closer . . .

That was when the shot rang out. The hyenas bolted into the long grass, and were gone. When Bertie turned around he saw his mother in her nightgown, rifle in hand, running toward him down the hill. He had never seen her run before. Between them they gathered up the mud-matted cub and brought him home. He was too weak to struggle, though he tried. As soon as they had given him some warm milk, they dunked him in the bath to wash him. As the first of the mud came off, Bertie saw he was white underneath.

"You see!" he cried triumphantly. "He *is* white! He *is*. I told you, didn't I? He's my white lion!" His mother still could not bring herself to believe it. Five baths later, she had to.

They sat him down by the stove in a washing basket and fed him again, all the milk he could drink. Then he lay down and slept. He was still asleep when Bertie's father got back at lunch time. They told him how it had all happened.

"Please, Father. I want to keep him," Bertie said.

"And so do I," said his mother. "We both do." And she spoke as Bertie had never heard her speak before, her voice strong, determined.

Bertie's father didn't seem to know how to reply. He just said, "We'll talk about it later," and then he walked out.

They did talk about it later, when Bertie was supposed to be in bed. He wasn't, though. He'd heard them arguing. He was outside the sitting-room door, watching, listening. Bertie's father was pacing up and down.

"He'll grow up, you know," he was saying. "You can't keep a grown lion, you know that."

"And *you* know we can't just throw him to the hyenas," replied his mother. "He needs us, and maybe we need him. He'll be someone for Bertie to play with for a while." And then she added sadly, "After all, it's not as if he's going to have any brothers and sisters, is it?"

At this, Bertie's father went over to her and kissed her gently on the forehead. It was the only time Bertie had ever seen him kiss her.

"All right then," he said. "All right. You can keep your lion."

So the white lion cub came to live with them in the farmhouse. He slept at the end of Bertie's bed. Wherever Bertie went, the lion cub went too—even to the bathroom, where he would watch Bertie have his bath and lick his legs dry afterward. They were never apart. It was Bertie who saw to the feeding—

milk four times a day from one of his father's beer bottles—until later on when the lion cub lapped from a soup bowl. There was impala meat whenever he wanted it, and as he grew—and he grew fast—he wanted more and more of it.

For the first time in his life Bertie was totally happy. The lion cub was all the brothers and sisters he could ever want, all the friends he could ever need. The two of them would sit side by side on the sofa out on the veranda and watch the great red sun go down over Africa, and Bertie would read him *Peter and the Wolf,* and at the end he would always promise him that he would never let him go off to a zoo and live behind bars like the wolf in the story. And the lion cub would look at Bertie with his trusting amber eyes.

"Why don't you give him a name?" his mother asked one day.

"Because he doesn't need one," replied Bertie. "He's a lion, not a person. Lions don't need names."

Bertie's mother was always wonderfully patient with the lion, no matter how much mess he made, how many cushions he pounced on and ripped apart. None of it seemed to upset her. And strangely, she was hardly ever ill these days. There was a spring to her step, and her laughter pealed through the house. His father was less happy about it. "Lions," he'd mutter, "should not live in houses. You should keep him outside in the compound." But they never did. For both mother and son, the lion had brought new life to their days, life and laughter.

Introduction

This wonderful book begins with these words:
"The Iron Giant came to the top of the cliff.
How far had he walked? Nobody knows.
Where had he come from? Nobody knows.
How was he made? Nobody knows."
The Iron Giant falls, shattering himself on the
rocks below. Bit by bit he pieces himself together,
all except for one ear, which he cannot find. Maybe
the sea has washed it away. He goes down to the
sea to look—down, down until the water covers
him completely. But we haven't seen the last
of the Iron Giant. In fact, the
story's just beginning.

THE IRON GIANT

TED HUGHES

The Return of the Iron Giant

From farm to farm, over the soft soil of the fields, went giant footprints, each one the size of a single bed.

The farmers, in a frightened, silent, amazed crowd, followed the footprints. And at every farm the footprints visited, all the metal machinery had disappeared.

Finally, the footprints led back up to the top of the cliff, where the little boy had seen the Iron Giant appear the night before, when he was fishing. The footprints led right to the cliff top.

And all the way down the cliff were torn marks on the rocks, where a huge iron body had slid down. Below, the tide was in. The gray, empty, moving tide. The Iron Giant had gone back into the sea.

SO

The furious farmers began to shout. The Iron Giant had stolen all their machinery. Had he eaten it? Anyway, he had taken it.

It had gone. What if he came again? What would he take next time? Cows? Houses? People?

They would have to do something.

They couldn't call in the police or the army, because nobody would believe them about this Iron Monster. They would have to do something for themselves.

So, what did they do?

At the bottom of the hill, below where the Iron Giant had come over the high cliff, they dug a deep, enormous hole. A hole wider than a house, and as deep as three trees one on top of the other. It was a colossal hole. A stupendous hole! And the sides of it were sheer as walls.

They pushed all the earth off to one side.

They covered the hole with branches and the branches were covered with straw and the straw with soil, so when they finished, the hole looked like a freshly plowed field.

Now, on the side of the hole opposite the slope up to the top of the cliff, they put an old rusty truck. That was the bait. Now they reckoned the Iron Giant would come over the top of the cliff out of the sea, and he'd see the old truck, which was painted red, and he'd come down to get it to chew it up and eat it. But on his way to the truck he'd be crossing the hole, and the moment he stepped with his great weight onto that soil held up only with straw and branches, he would crash through into the hole and would never get out. They'd find him there in the hole. Then they'd bring the few bulldozers and earth-movers that he hadn't already eaten, and they'd push the pile of earth in on top of him, and bury him forever in the hole. They were certain now that they'd get him.

Next morning, in great excitement, all the farmers gathered together to go along to examine their trap. They came carefully closer, expecting to see hands tearing at the edge of the pit. They came carefully closer.

The red truck stood just as they had left it. The soil lay just as they had left it, undisturbed. Everything was just as they had left it. The Iron Giant had not come.

Nor did he come that day.

Next morning, all the farmers came again. Still, everything lay just as they had left it.

And so it went on, day after day. Still the Iron Giant never came.

Now the farmers began to wonder if he would ever come again. They began to wonder if he had ever come at all. They began to make up explanations of what had happened to their machinery. Nobody likes to believe in an Iron Monster that eats tractors and cars.

Soon, the farmer who owned the red truck they were using as bait decided that he needed it, and he took it away. So there lay the beautiful deep trap, without any bait. Grass began to grow on the loose soil.

The farmers talked of filling the hole in. After all, you can't leave a giant pit like that, somebody might fall in. Some stranger coming along might just walk over it and fall in.

But they didn't want to fill it in. It had been such hard work digging it. Besides, they all had a sneaking fear that the Iron Giant might come again, and the hole was their only weapon against him.

At last they put up a little notice: DANGER: KEEP OFF, to warn people away, and they left it at that.

Now the little boy Hogarth had an idea. He thought he could use that hole to trap a fox. He found a dead hen one day, and threw it out on to the loose soil over the trap. Then toward evening, he climbed a tree nearby and waited. A long time he waited. A star came out. He could hear the sea.

Then—there, standing at the edge of the hole, was a fox. A big red fox, looking toward the dead hen. Hogarth stopped breathing. And the fox stood without moving—sniff, sniff, sniff, out toward the hen. But he did not step out onto the trap. Slowly, he walked around the wide patch of raw soil till he got back to where he'd started, sniffing all the time out toward the bird. But he did not step out onto the trap. Was he too smart to walk out there where it was not safe?

But at that moment he stopped sniffing. He turned his head and looked toward the top of the cliff. Hogarth, wondering what the fox had seen, looked toward the top of the cliff.

There, enormous in the blue evening sky, stood the Iron Giant, on the brink of the cliff, gazing inland.

In a moment, the fox had vanished.

Now what?

Hogarth carefully, quietly, hardly breathing, climbed slowly down the tree. He must get home and tell his father. But at the bottom of the tree he stopped. He could no longer see the Iron Giant against the twilight sky. Had he gone back over the cliff into the sea? Or was he coming down the hill, in the darkness under that high skyline, toward Hogarth and the farms?

Then Hogarth understood what was happening. He could hear a strange tearing and creaking sound. The Iron Giant was pulling up the barbed wire fence that led down the hill. And soon Hogarth could see him, as he came nearer, tearing the wire from the fence posts, rolling it up like spaghetti, and eating it. The Iron Giant was eating the barbed fencing wire.

But if he went along the fence, eating as he moved, he wouldn't come anywhere near the trap, which was out in the middle of the field. He could spend the whole night wandering about the countryside along the fences, rolling up the wire and eating it, and never would any fence bring him near the trap.

But Hogarth had an idea. In his pocket, among other things, he had a long nail and a knife. He took these out. Did he dare? His idea frightened him. In the silent dusk, he tapped the nail and the knife blade together.

Clink, Clink, Clink!

At the sound of the metal, the Iron Giant's hands became still. After a few seconds, he slowly turned his head and the headlight eyes shone toward Hogarth.

Again, Clink, Clink, Clink! went the nail on the knife.

Slowly, the Iron Giant took three strides toward Hogarth, and again stopped. It was now quite dark. The headlights shone red. Hogarth pressed close to the tree trunk. Between him and the Iron Giant lay the wide lid of the trap.

Clink, Clink, Clink! Again he tapped the nail on the knife.

And now the Iron Giant was coming. Hogarth could feel the earth shaking under the weight of his footsteps. Was it too late to run? Hogarth stared at the Iron Giant, looming, searching toward him for the taste of the metal that had made that inviting sound.

Clink, Clink, Clink! went the nail on the knife. And CRASSSHHH!

The Iron Giant vanished.

He was in the pit. The Iron Giant had fallen into the pit. Hogarth went close. The earth was shaking as the Iron Giant struggled underground. Hogarth peered over the torn edge of the great pit. Far below, two deep red headlights glared

up at him from the pitch blackness. He could hear the Iron Giant's insides grinding down there and it sounded like a big truck grinding its gears on a steep hill. Hogarth set off. He ran, he ran, home—home with the great news. And as he passed the cottages on the way, and as he turned down the lane toward his father's farm, he was shouting "The Iron Giant's in the trap!" and "We've caught the Iron Giant!"

Introduction

William Brown is a rogue—there's never been anyone like him. What is terrific about him is that he gets himself into all kinds of scrapes and always comes out smiling. He says just what he thinks, just what he feels. If he gets an idea in his head, it's always the best idea he's ever had, and he simply goes for it. And when things don't work out as he planned, there is always trouble, big trouble. But does William mind? Does William care? Of course not. He picks himself up and goes on being himself, being just William. That's why we love him.

JUST WILLIAM

RICHMAL CROMPTON

The Fall of the Idol

William was bored. He sat at his desk in the sunny schoolroom and gazed dispassionately at a row of figures on the blackboard.

"It isn't *sense*," he murmured scornfully.

Miss Drew was also bored, but, unlike William, she tried to hide the fact.

"If the interest on a hundred pounds for one year is five pounds," she said wearily, then, "William Brown, do sit up and don't look so stupid!"

William changed his position from that of lolling over one side of his desk to that of lolling over the other, and began to justify himself.

"Well, I can't unner*stand* any of it. It's enough to make anyone look stupid when he can't unner*stand* any of it. I can't think why

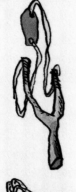

people go on givin' people bits of money for givin' 'em lots of money and go on an' on doin' it. It dun't seem sense. Anyone's a mug for givin' anyone a hundred pounds just 'cause he says he'll go on givin' him five pounds and go on stickin' to his hundred pounds. How's he to *know* he will? Well," he warmed to his subject, "what's to stop him not givin' any five pounds once he's got hold of the hundred pounds an' goin' on stickin' to the hundred pounds—"

Miss Drew checked him by a slim, upraised hand.

"William," she said patiently, "just listen to me. Now suppose," her eyes roved round the room and settled on a small red-haired boy, "suppose that Eric wanted a hundred pounds for something and you lent it to him—"

"I wun't lend Eric a hundred pounds," he said firmly, "'cause I ha'n't got it. I've only got 3½ pence, an' I wun't lend that to Eric, 'cause I'm not such a mug, 'cause I lent him my mouth-organ once an' he bit a bit off an'—"

Miss Drew interrupted sharply. Teaching on a hot afternoon is rather trying.

"You'd better stay in after school, William, and I'll explain."

William scowled, emitted his monosyllable of scornful disdain "Huh!" and relapsed into gloom.

He brightened, however, on remembering a lizard he had caught on the way to school, and drew it from its hiding place in his pocket. But the lizard had abandoned the unequal struggle for existence among the stones, top, penknife, bits of putty, and other small objects that inhabited William's pocket. The housing problem had been too much for it.

William, in disgust, shrouded the remains in blotting paper, and disposed of it in his neighbor's inkstand. The neighbor protested and an enlivening scrimmage ensued.

Finally the lizard was dropped down the neck of an inveterate enemy of William's in the next row, and was extracted only with the help of obliging friends. Threats of vengeance followed, couched in bloodcurdling terms, and written on blotting paper.

Meanwhile, Miss Drew explained Simple Practice to a small, but earnest, coterie of admirers in the front row. And William, in the back row, whiled away the hours for which his father paid the education authorities a substantial sum.

But his turn was to come.

At the end of afternoon school one by one the class departed, leaving William only nonchalantly chewing an india rubber and glaring at Miss Drew.

"Now, William."

Miss Drew was severely patient.

William went up to the platform and stood by her desk.

"You see, if someone borrows a hundred pounds from someone else—"

She wrote down the figures on a piece of paper, bending low over her desk. The sun poured in through the window, showing the little golden curls in the nape of her neck. She lifted to William eyes that were stern and frowning, but blue as blue above flushed cheeks.

"Don't you *see*, William?" she said.

There was a faint perfume about her, and William the devil-may-care pirate and robber-chief, the stern despiser of all

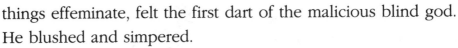

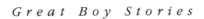

things effeminate, felt the first dart of the malicious blind god. He blushed and simpered.

"Yes, I see all about it now," he assured her. "You've explained it all plain now. I cudn't unner*stand* it before. It's a bit soft—in't it—anyway, to go lending hundred pounds about just 'cause someone says they'll give you five pounds next year. Some folks is mugs. But I do unner*stand* now. I cudn't unnerstand it before."

"You'd have found it simpler if you hadn't played with dead lizards all the time," she said wearily, closing her books.

William gasped.

He went home her devoted slave. Certain members of the class always deposited dainty bouquets on her desk in the morning. William was determined to outshine the rest. He went into the garden with a large basket and a pair of scissors the next morning before he set out for school.

It happened that no one was about. He went first to the greenhouse. It was a riot of color. He worked there with a thoroughness and concentration worthy of a nobler cause.

He came out staggering beneath a piled-up basket of greenhouse blooms. The greenhouse itself was bare and desolate.

Hearing a sound in the back garden he hastily decided to delay no longer, but to set out to school at once. He set out as unostentatiously as possible.

Miss Drew, entering her classroom, was aghast to see instead of the usual small array of buttonholes on her desk, a mass of already withering greenhouse flowers completely covering her desk and chair.

William was a boy who never did things by halves.

"Good Heavens!" she cried in consternation.

William blushed with pleasure.

He changed his seat to one in the front row. All that morning he sat, his eyes fixed on her earnestly, dreaming of moments in which he rescued her from robbers and pirates (here he was somewhat inconsistent with his own favorite role of robber-chief and pirate), and bore her, fainting in his strong arms, to safety. Then she clung to him in love and gratitude, and they were married at once by the Archbishops of Canterbury and York.

William would have no half-measures. They were to be married by the Archbishops of Canterbury and York, or else the Pope. He wasn't sure that he wouldn't rather have the Pope. He would wear his black pirate suit with the skull and crossbones. No, that would not do—

"What have I just been saying, William?" said Miss Drew.

William coughed and gazed at her soulfully.

"'Bout lendin' money?" he said, hopefully.

"William!" she snapped. "This isn't an arithmetic lesson. I'm trying to teach you about the Armada."

"Oh, *that*!" said William brightly and ingratiatingly. "Oh, yes."

"Tell me something about it."

"I don't *know* anything—not jus' yet—"

"I've been *telling* you about it. I do wish you'd listen," she said despairingly.

William relapsed into silence, nonplussed, but by no means cowed.

When he reached home that evening he found that the garden was the scene of excitement and hubbub. One policeman was measuring the panes of glass in the conservatory door, and another was on his knees examining the beds near. His grown-up sister, Ethel, was standing at the front door.

"Every single flower has been stolen from the conservatory some time this morning," she said excitedly. "We've only just been able to get the police. William, did you see anyone about when you went to school this morning?"

William pondered deeply. His most guileless and innocent expression came to his face.

"No," he said at last. "No, Ethel, I didn't see nobody."

William coughed and discreetly withdrew.

That evening he settled down at the library table, spreading out his books around him, a determined frown upon his small face.

His father was sitting in an armchair by the window reading the evening paper.

"Father," said William suddenly, "s'pose I came to you an' said you was to give me a hundred pounds an' I'd give you five pounds next year an' so on, would you give it me?"

"I should not, my son," said his father firmly.

William sighed.

"I knew there was something wrong with it," he said.

Mr. Brown returned to the leading article, but not for long.

"Father, what was the date of the Armada?"

"Good Heavens! How should I know? I wasn't there."

William sighed.

"Well, I'm tryin' to write about it and why it failed an'—why did it fail?"

Mr. Brown groaned, gathered up his paper, and retired to the dining room.

He had almost finished the leading article when William appeared, his arms full of books, and sat down quietly at the table.

"Father, what's the French for 'my aunt is walking in the garden'?"

"What on earth are you doing?" said Mr. Brown irritably.

"I'm doing my homework," said William virtuously.

"I never even knew you had it to do."

"No," William admitted gently, "I don't generally take much bother over it, but I'm goin' to now—'cause Miss Drew"— he blushed slightly and paused—"'cause Miss Drew"—he blushed more deeply and began to stammer, "'c-cause Miss Drew"—he was almost apoplectic.

Mr. Brown quietly gathered up his paper and crept out to the veranda, where his wife sat with the week's mending.

"William's gone raving mad in the dining room," he said pleasantly, as he sat down. "Takes the form of a wild thirst for knowledge, and a babbling of a Miss Drawing, or Drew, or something. He's best left alone."

Mrs. Brown merely smiled placidly over the mending.

Mr. Brown had finished one leading article and begun another before William appeared again. He stood in the doorway frowning and stern.

"Father, what's the capital of Holland?"

"Good Heavens!" said his father. "Buy him an encyclopedia. Anything, anything. What does he think I am? What—"

"I'd better set apart a special room for his homework," said Mrs. Brown soothingly, "now that he's beginning to take such an interest."

"A room!" echoed his father bitterly. "He wants a whole house."

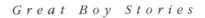

Miss Drew was surprised and touched by William's earnestness and attention the next day. At the end of the afternoon school he kindly offered to carry her books home for her. He waved aside all protests. He marched home by her side discoursing pleasantly, his small freckled face beaming devotion.

"I like pirates, don't you, Miss Drew? An' robbers an' things like that? Miss Drew, would you like to be married to a robber?"

He was trying to reconcile his old beloved dream of his future estate with the new one of becoming Miss Drew's husband.

"No," she said firmly.

His heart sank.

"Nor a pirate?" he said sadly.

"No."

"They're quite nice really—pirates," he assured her.

"I think not."

"Well," he said resignedly, "we'll jus' have to go huntin' wild animals and things. That'll be all right."

"Who?" she said, bewildered.

"Well—jus' you wait," he said darkly.

Then: "Would you rather be married by the Archbishop of York or the Pope?"

"The Archbishop, I think," she said gravely.

He nodded.

"All right."

Introduction

*I don't know how many books have been written
about King Arthur. Hundreds probably—I've written
one myself. But this must be the best one of them
all, and it's certainly the funniest.*

*Two boys, the Wart (nickname for Art, which
is short for Arthur) and Kay, grow up in a castle
"in an enormous clearing in a still more enormous
forest" with their father, Sir Ector. Kay is his real son,
the Wart is his adopted son. One day Sir Ector decides
he must start a quest to find a tutor for the two boys.
Then by chance, after he has been hawking and is
alone and lost in the forest, the Wart meets an old
man with a long, white beard and a long, white
mustache. It is the wizard Merlyn, who is
to become his tutor and change his whole life.*

THE SWORD IN THE STONE

T. H. WHITE

Merlyn took off his pointed hat when he came into this extraordinary chamber, because it was too high for the roof, and immediately there was a little scamper in one of the dark corners and a flap of soft wings, and a young tawny owl was sitting on the black skull-cap which protected the top of his head.

"Oh, what a lovely owl!" cried the Wart.

But when he went up to it and held out his hand, the owl grew half as tall again, stood up as stiff as a poker, closed its eyes so that there was only the smallest slit to peep through, as one is in the habit of doing when told to shut one's eyes at hide-and-seek, and said in a doubtful voice:

"There is no owl."

Then it shut its eyes entirely and looked the other way.

"It's only a boy," said Merlyn.

"There is no boy," said the owl hopefully, without turning round.

The Wart was so startled by finding that the owl could talk that he forgot his manners and came closer still. At this the owl became so nervous that it made a mess on Merlyn's head—the whole room was quite white with droppings—and flew off to perch on the farthest tip of the corkindrill's tail, out of reach.

"We see so little company," explained Merlyn, wiping his head with half a worn-out pair of pajama tops which he kept for that purpose, "that Archimedes is a little shy of strangers. Come, Archimedes, I want you to meet a friend of mine called Wart."

Here he held out his hand to the owl, who came waddling like a goose along the corkindrill's back—he waddled with this rolling gait so as to keep his tail from being damaged—and hopped down on to Merlyn's finger with every sign of reluctance.

"Hold out your finger," said Merlyn, "and put it behind his legs. No, lift it up under his train."

When the Wart had done this Merlyn moved the owl gently backwards, so that the Wart's finger pressed against its legs from behind, and it either had to step back on the finger or get pushed off its balance altogether. It stepped back. The Wart stood there delighted, while the furry little feet held tight on to his finger and the sharp claws prickled his skin.

"Say how d'you do properly," said Merlyn.

"I won't," said Archimedes, looking the other way and holding very tight.

"Oh, he *is* lovely," said the Wart again. "Have you had him very long?"

"Archimedes has stayed with me since he was quite small, indeed since he had a tiny head like a chicken's."

"I wish he would talk to me," said the Wart.

"Perhaps if you were to give him this mouse here, politely, he might learn to know you better."

Merlyn took a dead mouse out of his skull-cap—"I always keep them there," he explained, "and worms, too, for fishing. I find it most convenient"—and handed it to the Wart, who held it out rather gingerly towards Archimedes. The nutty little curved beak looked as if it were capable of doing damage, but Archimedes looked closely at the mouse, blinked at the Wart, moved nearer on the finger, closed his eyes and leaned forward. He stood there with closed eyes and an expression of rapture on his face, as if he were saying grace, and then, with the absurdest little sideways nibble, took the morsel so gently that he would not have broken a soap bubble. He remained leaning forward with closed eyes, with the mouse suspended from his beak, as if he were not sure what to do with it. Then he lifted his right foot—he was right-handed—and took hold of the mouse. He held it up like a boy holding a stick of rock or a constable with his truncheon, looked at it, nibbled its tail. He turned it round so that it was head first, for the Wart had offered it the wrong way round, and gave one gulp. He looked round at the company with the tail hanging out of the corner of his mouth—as much as to say, "I wish you would not all stare at me so"—turned his head away, politely swallowed the tail, scratched his sailor's beard with his left toe, and began to ruffle out his feathers.

"Let him alone," said Merlyn, "now. For perhaps he does not want to be friends with you until he knows what you are like. With owls, it is never easy-come and easy-go."

"Perhaps he will sit on my shoulder," said the Wart, and with that he instinctively lowered his hand, so that the owl, who liked to be as high as possible, ran up the slope and stood shyly beside his ear.

"Now breakfast," said Merlyn.

The Wart saw that the most perfect breakfast was laid out
neatly for two, on a table before the window. There were
peaches. There were also melons, strawberries and cream, rusks,
brown trout piping hot, grilled perch which were much nicer,
chicken devilled enough to burn one's mouth out, kidneys and
mushrooms on toast, fricassee, curry, and a choice of boiling
coffee or best chocolate made with cream in large cups.

"Have some mustard," said Merlyn, when they had got to
the kidneys.

The mustard-pot got up and walked over to his plate on thin
silver legs that waddled like the owl's. Then it uncurled its handles
and one handle lifted its lid with exaggerated courtesy while the
other helped him to a generous spoonful.

"Oh, I love the mustard-pot!" cried the Wart. "Where ever did
you get it?"

At this the pot beamed all over its face and began to strut a bit; but Merlyn rapped it on the head with a teaspoon, so that it sat down and shut up at once.

"It's not a bad pot," he said grudgingly. "Only it is inclined to give itself airs."

The Wart was so much impressed by the kindness of the old magician, and particularly by all the lovely things which he possessed, that he hardly liked to ask him personal questions. It seemed politer to sit still and speak when he was spoken to. But Merlyn did not speak very much, and when he did speak it was never in questions, so that the Wart had little opportunity for conversation. At last his curiosity got the better of him, and he asked something which had been puzzling him for some time.

"Would you mind if I ask you a question?"

"It is what I am for," said Merlyn sadly.

"How did you know to set the breakfast for two?"

The old gentleman leaned back in his chair and lightedt an enormous meerschaum pipe—Good gracious, he breathes fire, thought the Wart, who had never heard of tobacco—before he was ready to reply. Then he looked puzzled, took off his skull-cap—three mice fell out—and scratched in the middle of his bald head.

"Have you ever tried to draw in a looking-glass?" asked Merlyn.

"I don't think I have," said the Wart.

"Looking-glass," said the old gentleman, holding out his hand. Immediately there was a tiny lady's vanity-glass in his hand.

"Not that kind, you fool," said Merlyn angrily. "I want one big enough to shave in."

The vanity-glass vanished, and in its place there was a shaving mirror about a foot square. Merlyn then demanded pencil and paper in quick succession; got an unsharpened pencil and the *Morning Post*; sent them back; got a fountain pen with no ink in it and six reams of brown paper suitable for parcels; sent them back; flew into a passion in which he said by-our-lady quite often, and ended up with a carbon pencil and some cigarette papers which he said would have to do.

He put one of the papers in front of the glass and made five dots on it like this:

"Now," he said, "I want you to join those five dots up to make a W, looking only in the glass."

The Wart took the pen and tried to do as he was bid, but after a lot of false starts the letter which he produced was this:

"Well, it isn't bad," said Merlyn doubtfully, "and in a way it does look a bit like an M."

Then he fell into a reverie, stroking his beard, breathing fire, and staring at the paper.

"About the breakfast?" asked the Wart timidly, after he had waited five minutes.

"Ah, yes," said Merlyn. "How did I know to set breakfast for two? That was why I showed you the looking-glass. Now ordinary people are born *forwards* in Time, if you understand what I mean, and nearly everything in the world goes forward too. This makes it quite easy for the ordinary people to live, just as it would be easy to join those five dots into a W if you were allowed to look at them forwards instead of backwards and inside out. But I unfortunately was born at the wrong end of time, and I have to live *backwards* from in front, while surrounded by a lot of people living forwards from behind. Some people call it having second sight."

Merlyn stopped talking and looked at the Wart in an anxious way.

"Have I told you this before?" he inquired suspiciously.

"No," said the Wart. "We only met about half an hour ago."

"So little time to pass as that?" said Merlyn, and a big tear ran down to the end of his nose. He wiped it off with his pajama tops and added anxiously, "Am I going to tell it you again?"

"I don't know," said the Wart, "unless you haven't finished telling me yet."

"You see," said Merlyn, "one gets confused with Time, when it is like that. All one's tenses get muddled up, for one thing. If you know what's *going* to happen to people, and not what *has* happened to them, it makes it so difficult to prevent it happening, if you don't want it to have happened, if you see what I mean? Like drawing in a mirror."

The Wart did not quite see, but was just going to say that he was sorry for Merlyn if those things made him unhappy, when he felt a curious sensation at his ear. "Don't jump," said Merlyn, just as he was going to do so, and the Wart sat still. Archimedes, who had been standing forgotten on his shoulder all this time, was gently touching himself against him. His beak was right against the lobe of the ear, which its bristles made to tickle, and suddenly a soft hoarse little voice whispered, "How d'you do," so that it sounded right inside his head.

"Oh, owl!" cried the Wart, forgetting about Merlyn's troubles instantly. "Look, he has decided to talk to me!"

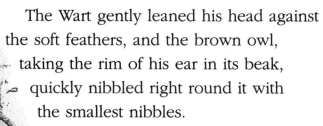

The Wart gently leaned his head against the soft feathers, and the brown owl, taking the rim of his ear in its beak, quickly nibbled right round it with the smallest nibbles.

"I shall call him Archie!" exclaimed the Wart.

"I trust you will do nothing of the sort," cried Merlyn instantly, in a stern and angry voice, and the owl withdrew to the farthest corner of his shoulder.

"Is it wrong?"

"You might as well call me Wol, or Olly," said the owl sourly, "and have done with it."

"Or Bubbles," added the owl in a bitter voice.

Merlyn took the Wart's hand and said kindly, "You are only young, and do not understand these things. But you will learn that owls are the politest and most courteous, single-hearted and faithful creatures living. You must never be familiar, rude or vulgar with them, or make them to look ridiculous. Their mother is Athene, the goddess of wisdom, and, though they are often ready to play the buffoon for your amusement, such conduct is the prerogative of the truly wise. No owl can possibly be called Archie."

"I am sorry, owl," said the Wart.

"And I am sorry, boy," said the owl. "I can see that you spoke in ignorance, and I bitterly regret that I should have been so petty as to take offense where none was intended."

The owl really did regret it, and looked so remorseful and upset that Merlyn had to put on a very cheerful manner and change the conversation.

"Well," said he, "now that we have finished breakfast, I think it is high time that we should all three find our way back to Sir Ector."

"Excuse me a moment," he added as an afterthought, and, turning round to the breakfast things, he pointed a knobbly finger at them and said in a stern voice, "Wash up."

At this all the china and cutlery scrambled down off the table, the cloth emptied the crumbs out of the window, and the napkins folded themselves up. All ran off down the ladder, to where Merlyn had left the bucket, and there was such a noise and yelling as if a lot of children had been let out of school. Merlyn went to the door and shouted, "Mind, nobody is to get broken." But his voice was entirely drowned in shrill squeals, splashes, and cries of "My, it is cold," "I shan't stay in long," "Look out, you'll break me," or "Come on, let's duck the teapot."

"Are you really coming all the way home with me?" asked the Wart, who could hardly believe the good news.

"Why not?" said Merlyn. "How else can I be your tutor?"

At this the Wart's eyes grew rounder and rounder, until they were about as big as the owl's who was sitting on his shoulder, and his face got redder and redder, and a big breath seemed to gather itself beneath his heart.

"My!" exclaimed the Wart, while his eyes sparkled with excitement at the discovery. "I must have been on a Quest."

Introduction

Peter, Susan, Edmund, and Lucy have all been
sent to the English countryside to escape the air raids
during World War II. They are living in a huge
house with many corridors and spare rooms.
In one of these rooms Lucy finds a wardrobe, climbs
into it, and finds herself in the magical land of Narnia.
Soon all of them are there, caught up in a titanic
struggle between the noble Aslan and the
White Witch—a struggle between good and evil in
which Peter must now play his part. The White Witch
has captured Edmund. With Aslan, Peter must
save him and defeat the White Witch.

THE LION, THE WITCH AND THE WARDROBE

C. S. LEWIS

Peter's First Battle

Aslan stood in the center of a crowd of creatures who had grouped themselves round him in the shape of a half-moon. There were Tree-Women there and Well-Women (Dryads and Naiads as they used to be called in our world) who had stringed instruments; it was they who had made the music. There were four great centaurs. The horse part of them was like huge English farm horses, and the man part was like stern but beautiful giants. There was also a unicorn, and a bull with the head of a man, and a pelican, and an eagle, and a great Dog. And next to Aslan stood two leopards of whom one carried his crown and the other his standard.

But as for Aslan himself, the Beavers and the children didn't know what to do or say when they saw him. People who have not been in Narnia sometimes think that a thing cannot be good

and terrible at the same time. If the children had ever thought so, they were cured of it now. For when they tried to look at Aslan's face they just caught a glimpse of the golden mane and the great, royal, solemn, overwhelming eyes; and then they found they couldn't look at him and went all trembly.

"Go on," whispered Mr. Beaver.

"No," whispered Peter, "you first."

"No, Sons of Adam before animals," whispered Mr. Beaver back again.

"Susan," whispered Peter, "what about you? Ladies first."

"No, you're the eldest," whispered Susan. And of course the longer they went on doing this the more awkward they felt. Then at last Peter realized that it was up to him. He drew his sword and raised it to the salute and hastily saying to the others "Come on. Pull yourselves together," he advanced to the Lion and said:

"We have come—Aslan."

"Welcome, Peter, Son of Adam," said Aslan. "Welcome, Susan and Lucy, Daughters of Eve. Welcome He-Beaver and She-Beaver."

His voice was deep and rich and somehow took the fidgets out of them. They now felt glad and quiet and it didn't seem awkward to them to stand and say nothing.

"But where is the fourth?" asked Aslan.

"He has tried to betray them and joined the White Witch, O Aslan," said Mr. Beaver. And then something made Peter say,

"That was partly my fault, Aslan. I was angry with him and I think that helped him to go wrong."

And Aslan said nothing either to excuse Peter or to blame him but merely stood looking at him with his great unchanging eyes. And it seemed to all of them that there was nothing to be said.

"Please—Aslan," said Lucy, "can anything be done to save Edmund?"

"All shall be done," said Aslan. "But it may be harder than you think." And then he was silent again for some time. Up to that moment Lucy had been thinking how royal and strong and peaceful his face looked; now it suddenly came into her head that he looked sad as well. But next minute that expression was quite gone.

The Lion shook his mane and clapped his paws together ("Terrible paws," thought Lucy, "if he didn't know how to velvet them!") and said,

"Meanwhile, let the feast be prepared. Ladies, take these Daughters of Eve to the pavilion and minister to them."

When the girls had gone Aslan laid his paw—and though it was velveted it was very heavy—on Peter's shoulder and said, "Come, Son of Adam, and I will show you a far-off sight of the castle where you are to be King."

And Peter with his sword still drawn in his hand went with the Lion to the eastern edge of the hilltop. There a beautiful sight met their eyes. The sun was setting behind their backs. That meant that the whole country below them lay in the evening light—forest and hills and valleys and, winding away like a silver snake, the lower part of the great river. And beyond all this, miles away, was the sea, and beyond the sea the sky, full of clouds which were just turning rose color with the reflection of the sunset. But just where the land of Narnia met the sea—in fact, at the mouth of the great river—there was something on a little hill, shining. It was shining because it was a castle and of course the sunlight was reflected from all the windows which looked toward Peter and the sunset; but to Peter it looked like a great star resting on the seashore.

"That, O Man," said Aslan, "is Cair Paravel of the four thrones, in one of which you must sit as King. I show it to you because you are the firstborn and you will be High King over all the rest."

And once more Peter said nothing, for at that moment a strange noise woke the silence suddenly. It was like a bugle, but richer.

"It is your sister's horn," said Aslan to Peter in a low voice; so low as to be almost a purr, if it is not disrespectful to think of a Lion purring.

For a moment Peter did not understand. Then, when he saw all the other creatures start forward and heard Aslan say with a wave of his paw, "Back! Let the Prince win his spurs," he did understand, and set off running as hard as he could to the pavilion. And there he saw a dreadful sight.

The Naiads and Dryads were scattering in every direction. Lucy was running toward him as fast as her short legs would carry her and her face was as white as paper. Then he saw Susan make a dash for a tree, and swing herself up, followed by a huge gray beast. At first Peter thought it was a bear. Then he saw it looked like an Alsatian, though it was far too big to be a dog. Then he realized that it was a wolf—a wolf standing on its hind legs, with its front paws against the tree-trunk, snapping and snarling. All the hair on its back stood up on end. Susan had not been able to get

higher than the second big branch. One of her legs hung down so that her foot was only an inch or two above the snapping teeth. Peter wondered why she did not get higher or at least take a better grip; then he realized that she was just going to faint and that if she fainted she would fall off.

Peter did not feel very brave; indeed, he felt he was going to be sick. But that made no difference to what he had to do. He rushed straight up to the monster and aimed a slash of his sword at its side. That stroke never reached the Wolf. Quick as lightning it turned round, its eyes flaming, and its mouth wide open in a howl of anger. If it had not been so angry that it simply had to howl it would have got him by the throat at once. As it was—though all this happened too quickly for Peter to think at all—he had just time to duck down and plunge his sword, as hard as he could, between the brute's forelegs into its heart. Then came a horrible, confused moment like something in a nightmare. He was tugging and pulling and the Wolf seemed neither alive nor dead, and its bared teeth knocked against his forehead, and everything was blood and heat and hair. A moment later he found that the monster lay dead and he had drawn his sword out of it and was straightening his back and rubbing the sweat off his face and out of his eyes. He felt tired all over.

Then, after a bit, Susan came down the tree. She and Peter felt pretty shaky when they met and I won't say there wasn't kissing and crying on both sides. But in Narnia no one thinks any the worse of you for that.

"Quick! Quick!" shouted the voice of Aslan. "Centaurs! Eagles! I see another wolf in the thickets. There—behind you. He has just darted away. After him, all of you. He will be going to his mistress. Now is your chance to find the Witch and rescue the fourth Son of Adam." And instantly with a thunder of hoofs and

beating of wings a dozen or so of the swiftest creatures
disappeared into the gathering darkness.

Peter, still out of breath, turned and saw Aslan close at hand.

"You have forgotten to clean your sword," said Aslan.

It was true. Peter blushed when he looked at the bright blade
and saw it all smeared with the Wolf's hair and blood. He stooped
down and wiped it quite clean on the grass, and then wiped it
quite dry on his coat.

"Hand it to me and kneel, Son of Adam," said Aslan. And
when Peter had done so he struck him with the flat of the blade
and said, "Rise up, Sir Peter Wolf's-Bane. And, whatever happens,
never forget to wipe your sword."

Introduction

Exiled from his home—because his parents do not want him to catch the measles from his brother, Peter—Tom has to stay with his Uncle Alan and Aunt Gwen. It's a bleak house, a big, old place, now divided into apartments. Oddly, there's a grandfather clock on the stairs, which never chimes the right hours—it even chimes thirteen sometimes. There is no yard, nowhere to play. Tom's bored. He isn't sleeping well, either. One night, hearing the clock strike thirteen again, he gets up. He finds the house changed—carpets where there were none, different furniture around, and a maid scurrying past who does not seem to know he's there. There's a back door, which opens easily, and Tom steps into a huge garden with hyacinths, a sundial, and a greenhouse. It's no dream. It's real.

TOM'S MIDNIGHT GARDEN

PHILIPPA PEARCE

Through a Door

Every night now Tom slipped downstairs to the garden. At first he used to be afraid that it might not be there. Once, with his hand already upon the garden door to open it, he had turned back, sick with grief at the very thought of absence. He had not dared, then, to look; but, later the same night, he had forced himself to go again and open that door: there the garden was. It had not failed him.

He saw the garden at many times of its day, and at different seasons—its favourite season was summer, with perfect weather. In earliest summer hyacinths were still out in the crescent beds on the lawn, and wallflowers in the round ones. Then the hyacinths bowed and died; and the wallflowers were uprooted, and stocks and asters bloomed in their stead. There was a clipped box bush by the greenhouse, with a cavity like a great mouth cut into the side of it: this was stacked full of pots of geraniums in flower. Along the sundial path, heavy red poppies came out, and roses;

and, in summer dusk, the evening primroses glimmered like little moons. In the latest summer the pears on the wall were muffled in muslin bags for safe ripening.

Tom was not a gardener, however; his first interest in a garden, as Peter's would have been, was tree-climbing. He always remembered his first tree in this garden—one of the yews round the lawn. He had never climbed a yew before, and was inclined to think ever afterwards that yews were best.

The first branches grew conveniently low, and the main trunk had bosses and crevices. With the toes of his left foot fitted into one of these last, Tom curved his hands round the branch over his head. Then he gave a push, a spring and a strong haul on the arms: his legs and feet were dangling free, and the branch was under his chest, and then under his middle. He drew himself still farther forward, at the same time twisting himself expertly: now he was sitting on the bough, a man's height above ground.

The rest of the ascent was easy but interesting: sometimes among the spreading, outermost branches; sometimes working close to the main trunk. Tom loved the dry feel of the bark on the main trunk. In places the bark had peeled away, and then a deep pink showed beneath, as though the tree were skin and flesh beneath its brown.

Up he went—up and up, and burst at last from the dim interior into an openness of blue and fiery gold. The sun was the gold, in a blue sky. All round him was a spreading, tufted surface of evergreen. He was on a level with all the yew-tree tops round the lawn; nearly on a level with the top of the tall south wall.

Tom was on a level, too, with the upper windows of the house, just across the lawn from him. His attention was caught by a movement inside one of the rooms: it came, he saw, from the same maid he had once seen in the hall. She was dusting

a bedroom, and came now to the window to raise the sash and shake her duster outside. She looked casually across to the yew-trees as she did so, and Tom tried waving to her. It was like waving to the He in blind-man's-buff.

The maid went back into the depths of the room, to her dusting. She left the window open behind her, and Tom could now see more. There was someone else in the room besides the maid—someone who stood against the far wall, facing the window. The maid evidently spoke to her companion occasionally as she worked, for Tom could hear the faint coming and going of voices. He could not see the other figure at all clearly, except that it was motionless, and there was the whiteness and shape of a face that was always turned in his direction. That steadfastness of direction embarrassed Tom. Very gradually he began to draw his head downwards, and then suddenly ducked it below tree-level altogether.

Tom saw more people later, in the garden itself. He stalked

them warily, and yet—remembering his invisibility to the
house-maid—with a certain confidence too.

He was pretty sure that the garden was used more often
than he knew. He often had the feeling of people having just
gone—and an uncomfortable feeling, out of which he tried to
reason himself, again. and again, of someone who had *not* gone:
someone who, unobserved, observed him. It was a relief really
to see people, even when they ignored his presence: the maid,
the gardener, and a severe-looking woman in a long dress of
rustling purple silk, face to face with whom Tom once came
unexpectedly, on a corner. She cut him dead.

Visibility . . . invisibility . . . If he were invisible to the
people of the garden, he was not completely so at least to some
of the other creatures. How truly they saw him he could not say;
but birds cocked their heads at him, and flew away when he
approached.

And had he any bodily weight in this garden, or had he not?
At first, Tom thought not. When he climbed the yew-tree he had
been startled to feel that no bough swung beneath him, and not
a twig broke. Later—and this was a great disappointment to
him—he found that he could not, by the ordinary grasping and
pushing of his hand, open any of the doors in the garden, to
go through them. He could not push open the door of the
greenhouse or of the little heating-house behind it, or the door
in the south wall by the sundial.

The doors shut against Tom were a check upon his curiosity,
until he saw a simple way out: he would get through the
doorways that interested him by following at the heels of the
gardener. He regularly visited the greenhouse, the heating-house,
and used the south wall door.

Tom concentrated upon getting through the south wall door.

That entry promised to be the easiest, because the gardener went through so often, with his tools. There must be a tool-shed somewhere through there.

The gardener usually went through so quickly and shut the door so smartly behind him, that there was not time for anyone else to slip through as well. However, he would be slower with a wheelbarrow, Tom judged; and he waited patiently for that opportunity. Yet even then the man somehow only made a long arm to open the door ahead of the wheelbarrow, wheeled it very swiftly through, caught the door-edge with the toe of his boot as he passed and slammed the door in Tom's face.

Tom glared at the door that once more was his barrier. Once more, without hope, he raised his hand to the latch and pressed it. As usual, he could not move it: his fingers seemed to have no substance. Then, in anger, he pressed with all imaginable might: he knitted his brows, and brought all his will to bear upon the latch, until he felt that something had to happen. It did: his fingers began to go through the latch, as though the latch, and not his fingers, now, were without substance. His fingers went through the ironwork of the latch altogether, and his hand fell back into place by his side.

Tom stared down at that ever-memorable right hand. He felt it tenderly with his left, to see if it were bruised or broken: it was quite unhurt—quite as before. Then he looked at the latch: it looked as real as any latch he had ever seen anywhere.

Then the idea came to Tom that the door might be no more solid than the latch, if he really tried it.

Deliberately he set his side against the door, shoulder, hip and heel, and pressed. At first, nothing gave, either of himself or the door. Yet he continued the pressure, with still greater force and greater determination; and gradually he became aware of a strange

sensation, that at first he thought was a numbness all down his side—but no, it was not that.

"I'm going through," Tom gasped, and was seized with alarm and delight.

On the other side of the wall, the gardener had emptied his barrow-load of weeds and was sitting on the handle of his barrow, in front of a potting-shed, eating his midday dinner. If he had been able to see Tom at all he would have seen a most curious sight: a very thin slice of boy, from shoulder to foot, coming through a perfectly solid wooden door. At first the body came through   evenly from top to bottom; then, the upper part seemed to stop, and the bottom part came through in its entirety, legs first. Then one arm came through, then another. Finally, everything was through except the head.

The truth was that Tom was now a little lacking courage. The passing through the door of so much of his body had not been without enormous effort and peculiar, if indescribable, sensations. "I'm just resting a minute," said Tom's head, on the garden side of the door; yet he knew that he was really delaying because he was nervous. His stomach, for instance, had felt most uncomfortable as it passed through the door; what would the experience be like for his head—his eyes, his ears?

On the other hand—and the new idea was even worse than the old—supposing that, like a locomotive-engine losing steam-pressure, he lost his present force of body and will-power in this delay? Then, he would be unable to move either forwards or backwards. He would be caught here by the neck, perhaps for ever. And just supposing someone came along, on the far side of the wall, who by some evil chance *could* see him—supposing a whole company came: they would see an entirely defenceless stern sticking out—an invitation to ridicule and attack.

With a convulsive effort, eyes closed, lips sealed, Tom dragged his head through the door, and stood, dizzy, dazed, but whole, on the far side of it.

When his vision cleared, he saw that he was standing directly in front of the potting-shed and the gardener. Tom had never been front to front with the gardener before: he was a large-framed young man, with a weather-reddened face, and eyes the colour of the sky itself—they now looked straight through Tom and far away. Into his mouth he was putting the last fragments of a thick bacon-and-bread sandwich. He finished the sandwich, closed his eyes and spoke aloud: "For all good things I thank the Lord; and may He keep me from all the works of the Devil that he hurt me not."

He spoke with a country voice, clipping short his t's and widening his vowels, so that Tom had to listen attentively to understand him.

The gardener opened his eyes again, and, reaching behind him, brought out another sandwich. Tom wondered, in some surprise, whether he said grace after every sandwich. Perhaps he never knew how many he was going to eat.

The gardener went on eating, and Tom turned away to look around him. He was in an orchard, that also served for the keeping of hens, the pegging out of washing and the kindling of a bonfire. Beyond the orchard were meadows and trees, from among which rose the roofs of what must be a village.

While he looked, Tom was also keeping a sharp eye upon the gardener. When the man had really finished his meal he grasped the handles of his wheelbarrow, to return to his work in the garden. In a moment, Tom was beside him. He had not at all enjoyed the experience of going through a shut door, and he did not now intend to have to repeat it. This time there was

an easy way through: he got nimbly up into the empty barrow
and was wheeled back into the garden in comfort.

It was a long time before Tom literally forced his way
through a door again. Anyway, he had seen the orchard, and
that was enough in that direction; other doors could wait.
Meanwhile, he climbed the low wall at the bottom of the
garden and explored the wood beyond. On the third side of
the garden he wormed his way through the hedge again and
crossed the meadow. The only surprise there was the boundary:
a river, clear, gentle-flowing, shallow, and green with reeds
and water-plants.

The garden and its surroundings, then, were not, in
themselves, outside the natural order of things; nor was Tom
alarmed by his own unnatural abilities. Yet to some things his
mind came back again and again, troubled: the constant fine
weather, the rapid coming and going of the seasons and the
times of day, the feeling of being watched.

One night all his uneasiness came to a head. He had gone
from his bed in the flat upstairs and crept down to the hall
at about midnight, as usual; he had opened the garden door.
He had found for the first time that it was night, too, in the
garden. The moon was up, but clouds fled continuously across
its face. Although there was this movement in the upper air,
down below there was none: a great stillness lay within the
garden, and a heavier heat than at any noon. Tom felt it: he
unbuttoned his pyjama jacket and let it flap open as he walked.

One could smell the storm coming. Before Tom had reached
the bottom of the garden, the moon had disappeared, obscured
altogether by cloud. In its place came another light that seemed
instantaneously to split the sky from top to bottom, and a few
seconds later came the thunder.

Tom turned back to the house. As he reached the porch, the winds broke out into the lower air, with heavy rain and a deathly chilling of the temperature. Demons of the air seemed let loose in that garden; and, with the increasing frequency of the lightning, Tom could watch the foliage of the trees ferociously tossed and torn at by the wind, and, at the corner of the lawn, the tall, tapering fir-tree swinging to and fro, its ivy-wreathed arms struggling wildly in the tempest like the arms of a swaddling-child.

To Tom it seemed that the fir-tree swung more widely each time. "It can't be blown over," thought Tom. "Strong trees are not often blown over."

As if in answer to this, and while the winds still tore, there came the loudest thunder, with a flash of lightning that was not to one side nor even above, but seemed to come down into the garden itself, to the tree. The glare was blinding, and Tom's eyes closed against it, although only for a part of a second. When he opened them again, he saw the tree like one flame, and falling. In the long instant while it fell, there seemed to be a horrified silence of all the winds; and, in that quiet, Tom heard something—a human cry—an "Oh!" of the terror he himself felt. It came from above him—from the window of one of the upper rooms.

Then the fir-tree fell, stretching its length—although Tom did not know this until much later—along the grave-beds of the asparagus in the kitchen-garden. It fell in darkness and the resumed rushing of wind and rain.

Tom was shaken by what he had seen and heard. He went back into the house and shut the garden door behind him. Inside, the grandfather clock ticked peacefully; the hall was still. He wondered if perhaps he had only imagined what he had seen outside. He opened the door again, and looked out. The summer storm was still raging. The flashes of lightning were distant now:

they lit up the ugly gap in the trees round the lawn, where the fir-tree had stood.

The tree had fallen, that had been a sight terrible enough; but the cry from above troubled Tom more. On the next night came the greatest shock of all. He opened the garden door as usual, and surveyed the garden. At first, he did not understand what was odd in its appearance; then, he realized that its usual appearance was in itself an oddity. In the trees round the lawn there was no gap: the ivy-grown fir-tree still towered above them.

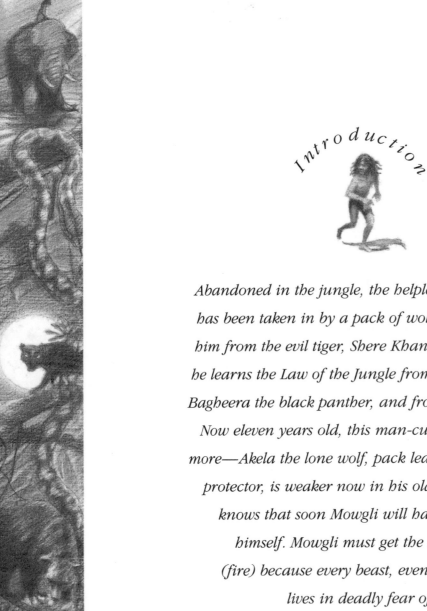

Introduction

Abandoned in the jungle, the helpless infant Mowgli has been taken in by a pack of wolves, which saved him from the evil tiger, Shere Khan. As he grows up, he learns the Law of the Jungle from the wolves, from Bagheera the black panther, and from Baloo the bear. Now eleven years old, this man-cub needs to learn more—Akela the lone wolf, pack leader, and Mowgli's protector, is weaker now in his old age. Bagheera knows that soon Mowgli will have to fend for himself. Mowgli must get the Red Flower (fire) because every beast, even Shere Khan, lives in deadly fear of it.

THE JUNGLE BOOK

RUDYARD KIPLING

Mowgli was far and far through the forest, running hard, and his heart was hot in him. He came to the cave as the evening mist rose, and drew breath, and looked down the valley. The cubs were out, but Mother Wolf, at the back of the cave, knew by his breathing that something was troubling her frog.

"What is it, Son?" she said.

"Some bat's chatter of Shere Khan," he called back. "I hunt among the ploughed fields tonight," and he plunged downward through the bushes, to the stream at the bottom of the valley. There he checked, for he heard the yell of the Pack hunting, heard the bellow of a hunted sambhur, and the snort as the buck turned at bay. Then there were wicked, bitter howls from the young wolves: "Akela! Akela! Let the Lone Wolf show his strength. Room for the leader of the Pack! Spring, Akela!"

The Lone Wolf must have sprung and missed his hold, for Mowgli heard the snap of his teeth and then a yelp as the sambhur knocked him over with his forefoot.

He did not wait for anything more, but dashed on; and the yells grew fainter behind him as he ran into the croplands where the villagers lived.

"Bagheera spoke truth," he panted, as he nestled down in some cattle-fodder by the window of a hut. "Tomorrow is one day both for Akela and for me."

Then he pressed his face close to the window and watched the fire on the hearth. He saw the husband-man's wife get up and feed it in the night with black lumps; and when the morning came and the mists were all white and cold, he saw the man's child pick up a wicker pot plastered inside with earth, fill it with lumps of red-hot charcoal, put it under his blanket, and go out to tend the cows in the byre.

"Is that all?" said Mowgli. "If a cub can do it, there is nothing to fear"; so he strode round the corner and met the boy, took the pot from his hand, and disappeared into the mist while the boy howled with fear.

"They are very like me," said Mowgli, blowing into the pot, as he had seen the woman do. "This thing will die if I do not give it things to eat"; and he dropped twigs and dried bark on the red stuff. Half-way up the hill he met Bagheera with the morning dew shining like moonstones on his coat.

"Akela has missed," said the Panther. "They would have killed him last night, but they needed thee also. They were looking for thee on the hill."

"I was among the ploughed lands. I am ready. See!" Mowgli held up the fire-pot.

"Good! Now, I have seen men thrust a dry branch into that

stuff, and presently the Red Flower blossomed at the end of it. Art thou not afraid?"

"No. Why should I fear? I remember now—if it is not a dream—how, before I was a Wolf, I lay beside the Red Flower, and it was warm and pleasant."

All that day Mowgli sat in the cave tending his fire-pot and dipping dry branches into it to see how they looked. He found a branch that satisfied him, and in the evening when Tabaqui came to the cave and told him rudely enough that he was wanted at the Council Rock, he laughed till Tabaqui ran away. Then Mowgli went to the Council, still laughing.

Akela the Lone Wolf lay by the side of his rock as a sign that the leadership of the Pack was open, and Shere Khan with his following of scrapfed wolves walked to and fro openly, being flattered. Bagheera lay close to Mowgli, and the fire-pot was between Mowgli's knees. When they were all gathered together, Shere Khan began to speak—a thing he would never have dared to do when Akela was in his prime.

"He has no right," whispered Bagheera. "Say so. He is a dog's son. He will be frightened."

Mowgli sprang to his feet. "Free People," he cried, "does Shere Khan lead the Pack? What has a tiger to do with our leadership?"

"Seeing that the leadership is yet open, and being asked to speak—" Shere Khan began.

"By whom?" said Mowgli. "Are we *all* jackals, to fawn on this cattle-butcher? The leadership of the Pack is with the Pack alone."

There were yells of "Silence, thou man's cub!" "Let him speak. He has kept our Law"; and at last the seniors of the Pack thundered: "Let the Dead Wolf speak." When a leader of the Pack has missed his kill, he is called the Dead Wolf as long as he lives, which is not long, as a rule.

Akela raised his old head wearily:

"Free People, and ye too, jackals of Shere Khan, for many seasons I have led ye to and from the kill, and in all my time not one has been trapped or maimed. Now I have missed my kill. Ye know how that plot was made. Ye know how ye brought me up to an untried buck to make my weakness known. It was cleverly done. Your right is to kill me here on the Council Rock now. Therefore, I ask, who comes to make an end of the Lone Wolf? For it is my right, by the Law of the Jungle, that ye come one by one."

There was a long hush, for no single wolf cared to fight Akela to the death. Then Shere Khan roared: "Bah! what have we to do with this toothless fool? He is doomed to die! It is the man-cub who has lived too long. Free People, he was my meat from the first. Give him to me. I am weary of this man-wolf folly. He has troubled the Jungle for ten seasons. Give me the man-cub, or I will hunt here always, and not give you one bone. He is a man, a man's child, and from the marrow of my bones I hate him!"

Then more than half the Pack yelled: "A man! a man! What has a man to do with us? Let him go to his own place."

"And turn all the people of the villages against us?" clamoured Shere Khan. "No; give him to me. He is a man, and none of us can look him between the eyes."

Akela lifted his head again, and said: "He has eaten our food. He has slept with us. He has driven game for us. He has broken no word of the Law of the Jungle."

"Also, I paid for him with a bull when he was accepted. The worth of a bull is little, but Bagheera's honour is something that he will perhaps fight for," said Bagheera, in his gentlest voice.

"A bull paid ten years ago!" the Pack snarled. "What do we care for bones ten years old?"

"Or for a pledge?" said Bagheera, his white teeth bared under his lip. "Well are ye called the Free People!"

"No man's cub can run with the people of the Jungle," howled Shere Khan. "Give him to me!"

"He is our brother in all but blood," Akela went on; "and ye would kill him here! In truth, I have lived too long. Some of ye are eaters of cattle, and of others I have heard that, under Shere Khan's teaching, ye go by dark night and snatch children from the villager's doorstep. Therefore I know ye to be cowards, and it is to cowards I speak. It is certain that I must die, and my life is of no worth, or I would offer that in the Man-cub's place. But for the sake of the honour of the Pack—a little matter that by being without a leader ye have forgotten—I promise that if ye let the Man-cub go to his own place, I will not, when my time comes to die, bare one tooth against ye. I will die without fighting. That will at least save the Pack three lives. More I cannot do; but if ye will, I can save ye the shame that comes of killing a brother against whom there is no fault—a brother spoken for and bought into the Pack according to the Law of the Jungle."

"He is a man—a man—a man!" snarled the Pack; and most of the wolves began to gather round Shere Khan, whose tail was beginning to switch.

"Now the business is in thy hands," said Bagheera to Mowgli. "*We* can do no more except fight."

Mowgli stood upright—the fire-pot in his hands. Then he stretched out his arms, and yawned in the face of the Council; but he was furious with rage and sorrow, for, wolf-like, the wolves had never told him how they hated him. "Listen, you!" he cried. "There is no need for this dog's jabber. Ye have told me so often tonight that I am a man (and indeed I would have been a wolf with you to my life's end), that I feel your words are true.

So I do not call ye my brothers any more, but *sag* [dogs], as a man should. What ye will do, and what ye will not do, is not yours to say. That matter is with *me;* and that we may see the matter more plainly, I, the man, have brought here a little of the Red Flower which ye, dogs, fear."

He flung the fire-pot on the ground, and some of the red coals lit a tuft of dried moss that flared up, as all the Council drew back in terror before the leaping flames.

Mowgli thrust his dead branch into the fire till the twigs lit and crackled, and whirled it above his head among the cowering wolves.

"Thou art the master," said Bagheera, in an undertone. "Save Akela from the death. He was ever thy friend."

Akela, the grim old wolf who had never asked for mercy in his life, gave one piteous look at Mowgli as the boy stood all naked, his long black hair tossing over his shoulders in the light of the blazing branch that made the shadows jump and quiver.

"Good!" said Mowgli, staring round slowly. "I see that ye are dogs. I go from you to my own people—if they be my own people. The Jungle is shut to me, and I must forget your talk and your companionship; but I will be more merciful than ye are. Because I was all but your brother in blood, I promise that when I am a man among men I will not betray ye to men as ye have betrayed me." He kicked the fire with his foot, and the sparks flew up. "There shall be no war between any of us and the Pack. But here is a debt to pay before I go." He strode forward to where Shere Khan sat blinking stupidly at the flames, and caught him by the tuft on his chin. Bagheera followed in case of accidents. "Up, dog!" Mowgli cried. "Up, when a man speaks, or I will set that coat ablaze!"

Shere Khan's ears lay flat back on his head, and he shut his eyes, for the blazing branch was very near.

"This cattle-killer said he would kill me in the Council because he had not killed me when I was a cub. Thus and thus, then, do we beat dogs when we are men. Stir a whisker, Lungri, and I ram the Red Flower down thy gullet!" He beat Shere Khan over the head with the branch, and the tiger whimpered and whined in an agony of fear.

"Pah! Singed jungle-cat—go now! But remember when next I come to the Council Rock, as a man should come, it will be with Shere Khan's hide on my head. For the rest, Akela goes free to live as he pleases. Ye will *not* kill him, because that is not my will. Nor do I think that ye will sit here any longer, lolling out your tongues as though ye were somebodies, instead of dogs whom I drive out —thus! Go!" The fire was burning furiously at the end of the branch, and Mowgli struck right and left round the circle, and the wolves ran howling with the sparks burning their fur. At last there were only Akela, Bagheera, and perhaps ten wolves that had taken Mowgli's part. Then something began to hurt Mowgli inside him, as he had never been hurt in his life before, and he caught his breath and sobbed, and the tears ran down his face.

"What is it? What is it?" he said. "I do not wish to leave the Jungle, and I do not know what this is. Am I dying, Bagheera?"

"No, Little Brother. Those are only tears such as men use," said Bagheera. "Now I know thou art a man, and a man's cub no longer. The Jungle is shut indeed to thee henceforward. Let them fall, Mowgli. They are only tears." So Mowgli sat and cried as though his heart would break; and he had never cried in all his life before.

"Now," he said, "I will go to men. But first I must say farewell to my mother"; and he went to the cave where she lived with Father Wolf, and he cried on her coat, while the four cubs howled miserably.

"Ye will not forget me?" said Mowgli.

"Never while we can follow a trail," said the cubs. "Come to the foot of the hill when thou art a man, and we will talk to thee; and we will come into the croplands to play with thee by night."

"Come soon!" said Father Wolf. "Oh, wise little frog, come again soon; for we be old, thy mother and I."

"Come soon," said Mother Wolf, "little naked son of mine; for, listen, child of man, I loved thee more than ever I loved my cubs."

"I will surely come," said Mowgli, "and when I come it will be to lay out Shere Khan's hide upon the Council Rock. Do not forget me! Tell them in the Jungle never to forget me!"

*Sam Gribley lives in an apartment in New York
with his mom, dad, four sisters, and four brothers.
None of them likes it, and Sam's dad hates it
more than all of them. It is from his dad that Sam
discovers where his great-grandfather came from—
the Catskill Mountains. He'd had a farm there.
"Somewhere in the Catskills is an old beech with the
name Gribley carved on it." That starts Sam thinking,
dreaming. In the New York Public Library he reads
about how to survive on the land. But Sam
doesn't just dream his dream of escape.
He lives his dream. He runs away.*

MY SIDE OF THE MOUNTAIN

JEAN CRAIGHEAD GEORGE

I left New York in May. I had a penknife, a ball of cord, an ax, and $40, which I had saved from selling magazine subscriptions. I also had some flint and steel which I had bought at a Chinese store in the city. The man in the store had showed me how to use it. He had also given me a little purse to put it in, and some tinder to catch the sparks. He had told me that if I ran out of tinder, I should burn cloth, and use the charred ashes.

I thanked him and said, "This is the kind of thing I am not going to forget."

On the train north to the Catskills I unwrapped my flint and steel and practiced hitting them together to make sparks. On the wrapping paper I made these notes.

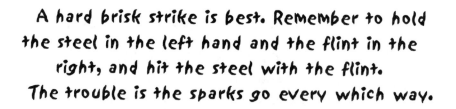

A hard brisk strike is best. Remember to hold the steel in the left hand and the flint in the right, and hit the steel with the flint. The trouble is the sparks go every which way.

And that *was* the trouble. I did not get a fire going that night, and as I mentioned, this was a scary experience.

I hitched rides into the Catskill Mountains. At about four o'clock a truck driver and I passed through a beautiful dark hemlock forest, and I said to him, "This is as far as I am going."

He looked all around and said, "You live here?"

"No," I said, "but I am running away from home, and this is just the kind of forest I have always dreamed I would run to. I think I'll camp here tonight." I hopped out of the cab.

"Hey, boy," the driver shouted. "Are you serious?"

"Sure," I said.

"Well, now, ain't that sumpin'? You know, when I was your age, I did the same thing. Only thing was, I was a farm boy and ran to the city, and you're a city boy running to the woods. I was scared of the city—do you think you'll be scared of the woods?"

"Heck, no!" I shouted loudly.

As I marched into the cool shadowy woods, I heard the driver call to me, "I'll be back in the morning, if you want to ride home."

He laughed. Everybody laughed at me. Even Dad. I told Dad that I was going to run away to Great-grandfather Gribley's land. He had roared with laughter and told me about the time he had run away from home. He got on a boat headed for Singapore, but when the whistle blew for departure, he was down the gangplank and home in bed before anybody knew he was gone. Then he told me, "Sure, go try it. Every boy should try it."

I must have walked a mile into the woods until I found a stream.

It was a clear athletic stream that rushed and ran and jumped and splashed. Ferns grew along its bank, and its rocks were upholstered with moss.

I sat down, smelled the piney air, and took out my penknife. I cut off a green twig and began to whittle. I have always been good at whittling. I carved a ship once that my teacher exhibited for parents' night at school.

First I whittled an angle on one end of the twig. Then I cut a smaller twig and sharpened it to a point. I whittled an angle on that twig, and bound the two angles face to face with a strip of green bark. It was supposed to be a fishhook.

According to a book on how to survive on the land that I read in the New York Public Library, this was the way to make your own hooks. I then dug for worms. I had hardly chopped the moss away with my ax before I hit frost. It had not occurred to me that there would be frost in the ground in May, but then, I had not been on a mountain before.

This did worry me, because I was depending on fish to keep me alive until I got to my great-grandfather's mountain, where I was going to make traps and catch game.

I looked into the stream to see what else I could eat, and as I did, my hand knocked a rotten log apart. I remembered about old logs and all the sleeping stages of insects that are in it. I chopped away until I found a cold white grub.

I swiftly tied a string to my hook, put the grub on, and walked up the stream looking for a good place to fish. All the manuals I had read were very emphatic about where fish lived, and so I had memorized this: "In streams, fish usually congregate in pools and deep calm water. The heads of riffles, small rapids, the tail of a pool, eddies below rocks or logs, deep undercut banks, in the shade of overhanging bushes—all are very likely places to fish."

This stream did not seem to have any calm water, and I must have walked a thousand miles before I found a pool by a deep undercut bank in the shade of overhanging bushes. Actually, it wasn't that far, it just seemed that way because as I went looking and finding nothing, I was sure I was going to starve to death.

I squatted on this bank and dropped in my line. I did so want to catch a fish. One fish would set me upon my way, because I had read how much you can learn from one fish. By examining the contents of its stomach you can find what the other fish are eating or you can use the internal organs as bait.

The grub went down to the bottom of the stream. It swirled around and hung still. Suddenly the string came to life, and rode back and forth and around in a circle. I pulled with a powerful jerk. The hook came apart, and whatever I had went circling back to its bed.

Well, that almost made me cry. My bait was gone, my hook was broken, and I was getting cold, frightened, and mad. I whittled another hook, but this time I cheated and used string to wind it together instead of bark. I walked back to the log and luckily found another grub. I hurried to the pool, and I flipped a trout out of the water before I knew I had a bite.

The fish flopped, and I threw my whole body over it. I could not bear to think of it flopping itself back into the stream.

I cleaned it like I had seen the man at the fish market do, examined its stomach, and found it empty. This horrified me. What I didn't know was that an empty stomach means the fish are hungry and will eat about anything. However, I thought at the time that I was a goner. Sadly, I put some of the internal organs on my hook, and before I could get my line to the bottom I had another bite. I lost that one, but got the next one. I stopped when I had five nice little trout and looked around for a place to build a camp and make a fire.

It wasn't hard to find a pretty spot along that stream. I selected a place beside a mossy rock in a circle of hemlocks.

I decided to make a bed before I cooked. I cut off some boughs for a mattress, then I leaned some dead limbs against the boulder and covered them with hemlock limbs. This made a kind of tent. I crawled in, lay down, and felt alone and secret and very excited.

But, ah, the rest of this story! I was on the northeast side of the mountain. It grew dark and cold early. Seeing the shadows slide down on me, I frantically ran around gathering firewood. This is about the only thing I did right from that moment until dawn, because I remembered that the driest wood in a forest is the dead limbs that are still on the trees, and I gathered an enormous pile of them. That pile must still be there, for I never

got a fire going.

I got sparks, sparks, sparks. I even hit the tinder with the sparks. The tinder burned all right, but that was as far as I got. I blew on it, I breathed on it, I cupped it in my hands, but no sooner did I add twigs than the whole thing went black.

Then it got too dark to see. I clicked steel and flint together, even though I couldn't see the tinder. Finally, I gave up and crawled into my hemlock tent, hungry, cold, and miserable.

I can talk about that first night now, although it is still embarrassing to me because I was so stupid, and scared, that I hate to admit it.

I had made my hemlock bed right in the stream valley where the wind drained down from the cold mountaintop. It might have been all right if I had made it on the other side of the boulder, but I didn't. I was right on the main highway of the cold winds as they tore down upon the valley below. I didn't have enough hemlock boughs under me, and before I had my head down, my stomach was cold and damp. I took some boughs off the roof and stuffed them under me, and then my shoulders were cold. I curled up in a ball and was almost asleep when a whippoorwill called. If you have ever been within forty feet of a whippoorwill, you will understand why I couldn't even shut my eyes. They are deafening!

Well, anyway, the whole night went like that. I don't think I slept fifteen minutes, and I was so scared and tired that my throat was dry. I wanted a drink but didn't dare go near the stream for fear of making a misstep and falling in and getting wet. So I sat tight, and shivered and shook—and now I am able to say—I cried a little tiny bit.

Fortunately, the sun has a wonderfully glorious habit of

rising every morning. When the sky lightened, when the birds awoke, I knew I would never again see anything so splendid as the round red sun coming up over the earth.

I was immediately cheered, and set out directly for the highway. Somehow, I thought that if I was a little nearer the road, everything would be all right.

I climbed a hill and stopped. There was a house. A house warm and cozy, with smoke coming out the chimney and lights in the windows, and only a hundred feet from my torture camp.

Without considering my pride, I ran down the hill and banged on the door. A nice old man answered. I told him everything in one long sentence, and then said, "And so, can I cook my fish here, because I haven't eaten in years."

He chuckled, stroked his whiskery face, and took the fish. He had them cooking in a pan before I knew what his name was.

When I asked him, he said Bill something, but I never heard his last name because I fell asleep in his rocking chair that was pulled up beside his big hot glorious wood stove in the kitchen.

I ate the fish some hours later, also some bread, jelly, oatmeal, and cream. Then he said to me, "Sam Gribley, if you are going to run off and live in the woods, you better learn how to make a fire. Come with me."

We spent the afternoon practicing. I penciled these notes on the back of a scrap of paper, so I wouldn't forget.

When the tinder glows, keep blowing and add fine dry needles one by one—and keep blowing, steadily, lightly, and evenly. Add one inch dry twigs to the needles and then give her a good big handful of small dry stuff.
Keep blowing.

The next day I told Bill good-bye, and as I strode, warm and fed, onto the road, he called to me, "I'll see you tonight. The back door will be open if you want a roof over your head."

I said, "Okay," but I knew I wouldn't see Bill again. I knew how to make fire, and that was my weapon. With fire I could conquer the Catskills. I also knew how to fish. To fish and to make a fire. That was all I needed to know, I thought.

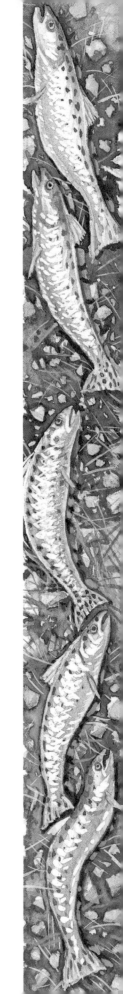

Introduction

All on board the Hispaniola *are bound for Treasure Island, but there's treachery afoot. Young Jim Hawkins, until now a great admirer of Long John Silver, climbs into a barrel to help himself to an apple. There he hears how Silver has nothing but mutiny and murder in his black heart, and how he plans to kill Captain Smollett and all of Jim's friends once they have found the treasure they seek. Trapped in the barrel, the worst is about to happen. It's Silver's voice, telling one of his cronies, ". . . you just jump up, like a sweet lad, and get me an apple. . . ." But Jim is saved in the nick of time by the look-out's shout of "Land ho!" Now he must alert Captain Smollett to the danger ahead. . . .*

TREASURE ISLAND

ROBERT LOUIS STEVENSON

Council of War

There was a great rush of feet across the deck. I could hear people tumbling up from the cabin and the foc's'le; and, slipping in an instant outside my barrel, I dived behind the foresail, made a double towards the stern, and came out upon the open deck in time to join Hunter and Dr. Livesey in the rush for the weather bow.

There all hands were already congregated. A belt of fog lifted almost simultaneously with the appearance of the moon. Away to the south-west of us we saw two low hills, about a couple of miles apart, and rising behind one of them a third and higher hill, whose peak was still buried in the fog. All three seemed sharp and conical in figure.

So much I saw, almost in a dream, for I had not yet recovered from my horrid fear of a minute or two before. And then I heard the voice of Captain Smollett issuing orders. The *Hispaniola* was laid a couple of points nearer the wind, and now sailed a course

that would just clear the island on the east.

"And now, men," said the captain, when all was sheeted home, "has any one of you ever seen that land ahead?"

"I have, sir," said Silver. "I've watered there with a trader I was cook in."

"The anchorage is on the south, behind an islet, I fancy?" asked the captain.

"Yes, sir; Skeleton Island they calls it. It were a main place for pirates once, and a hand we had on board knowed all their names for it. That hill to the nor'ard they calls the Fore-mast Hill; there are three hills in a row running south'ard—fore, main, and mizzen, sir. But the main—that's the big 'un, with the cloud on it—they usually calls the Spy-glass, by reason of a look-out they kept when they was in the anchorage cleaning; for it's there they cleaned their ships, sir, asking your pardon."

"I have a chart here," says Captain Smollett. "See if that's the place."

Long John's eyes burned in his head as he took the chart; but, by the fresh look of the paper, I knew he was doomed to disappointment. This was not the map we found in Billy Bones's chest, but an accurate copy, complete in all things—names and heights and soundings—with the single exception of the red crosses and the written notes. Sharp as must have been his annoyance, Silver had the strength of mind to hide it.

"Yes, sir," said he, "this is the spot to be sure; and very prettily drawn out. Who might have done that, I wonder? The pirates were too ignorant, I reckon. Ay, here it is: 'Capt. Kidd's Anchorage' —just the name my shipmate called it. There's a strong current runs along the south, and then away nor'ard up the west coast. Right you was, sir," says he, "to haul your wind and keep the weather of the island. Leastways, if such was your intention as to enter and careen, and there ain't no better place for that in these waters."

"Thank you, my man," says Captain Smollett. "I'll ask you, later on, to give us a help. You may go."

I was surprised at the coolness with which John avowed his knowledge of the island; and I own I was half-frightened when I saw him drawing nearer to myself. He did not know, to be sure, that I had overheard his council from the apple barrel, and yet I had, by this time, taken such a horror of his cruelty, duplicity, and power, that I could scarce conceal a shudder when he laid his hand upon my arm.

"Ah," says he, "this here is a sweet spot, this island—a sweet spot for a lad to get ashore on. You'll bathe, and you'll climb trees, and you'll hunt goats, you will; and you'll get aloft on them hills like a goat yourself. Why, it makes me young again. I was going to forget my timber leg, I was. It's a pleasant thing to be young, and have ten toes, and you may lay to that. When you want to go a bit of exploring, you just ask old John, and he'll put up a snack for you to take along."

And clapping me in the friendliest way upon the shoulder, he hobbled off forward and went below.

Captain Smollett, the squire, and Dr. Livesey were talking together on the quarter-deck, and, anxious as I was to tell them my story, I durst not interrupt them openly. While I was still casting about in my thoughts to find some probable excuse, Dr. Livesey called me to his side. He had left his pipe below, and being a slave to tobacco, had meant that I should fetch it; but as soon as I was near enough to speak and not to be overheard, I broke out immediately: "Doctor, let me speak. Get the captain and squire down to the cabin, and then make some pretence to send for me. I have terrible news."

The doctor changed countenance a little, but next moment he was master of himself.

"Thank you, Jim," said he, quite loudly, "that was all I wanted to know," as if he had asked me a question.

And with that he turned on his heel and rejoined the other two. They spoke together for a little, and though none of them started, or raised his voice, or so much as whistled, it was plain enough that Dr. Livesey had communicated my request; for the next thing that I heard was the captain giving an order to Job Anderson, and all hands were piped on deck.

"My lads," said Captain Smollett, "I've a word to say to you. This land that we have sighted is the place we have been sailing for. Mr. Trelawney, being a very open-handed gentleman, as we all know, has just asked me a word or two, and as I was able to tell him that every man on board had done his duty, alow and aloft, as I never ask to see it done better, why, he and I and the doctor are going below to the cabin to drink *your* health and luck, and you'll have grog served out for you to drink *our* health and luck. I'll tell you what I think of this: I think it handsome.

And if you think as I do, you'll give a good sea cheer for the gentleman that does it."

The cheer followed—that was a matter of course; but it rang out so full and hearty, that I confess I could hardly believe these same men were plotting for our blood.

"One more cheer for Cap'n Smollett," cried Long John, when the first had subsided.

And this also was given with a will.

On the top of that the three gentlemen went below, and not long after, word was sent forward that Jim Hawkins was wanted in the cabin.

I found them all three seated round the table, a bottle of Spanish wine and some raisins before them, and the doctor smoking away, with his wig on his lap, and that, I knew, was a sign that he was agitated. The stern window was open, for it was a warm night, and you could see the moon shining behind on the ship's wake.

"Now, Hawkins," said the squire, "you have something to say. Speak up."

I did as I was bid, and as short as I could make it, told the whole details of Silver's conversation. Nobody interrupted me till I was done, nor did any one of the three of them make so much as a movement, but they kept their eyes upon my face from first to last.

"Jim," said Dr. Livesey, "take a seat."

And they made me sit down at table beside them, poured me out a glass of wine, filled my hands with raisins, and all three, one after the other, and each with a bow, drank my good health, and their service to me, for my luck and courage.

"Now, captain," said the squire, "you were right, and I was wrong. I own myself an ass, and I await your orders."

"No more an ass than I, sir," returned the captain. "I never heard of a crew that meant to mutiny but what showed signs before, for any man that had an eye in his head to see the mischief and take steps according. But this crew," he added, "beats me."

"Captain," said the doctor, "with your permission, that's Silver. A very remarkable man."

"He'd look remarkably well from a yard-arm, sir," returned the captain. "But this is talk; this don't lead to anything. I see three or four points, and with Mr. Trelawney's permission, I'll name them."

"You, sir, are the captain. It is for you to speak," says Mr Trelawney, grandly.

"First point," began Mr. Smollett. "We must go on, because we can't turn back. If I gave the word to go about, they would rise at once. Second point, we have time before us—at least, until this treasure's found. Third point, there are faithful hands. Now, sir, it's got to come to blows sooner or later; and what I propose is, to take time by the forelock, as the saying is, and come to blows

some fine day when they least expect it. We can count, I take it, on your own home servants, Mr. Trelawney?"

"As upon myself," declared the squire.

"Three," reckoned the captain, "ourselves make seven, counting Hawkins, here. Now, about the honest hands?"

"Most likely Trelawney's own men," said the doctor; "those he had picked up for himself, before he lit on Silver."

"Nay," replied the squire, "Hands was one of mine."

"I did think I could have trusted Hands," added the captain.

"And to think that they're all Englishmen!" broke out the squire. "Sir, I could find it in my heart to blow the ship up."

"Well, gentlemen," said the captain, "the best that I can say is not much. We must lay to, if you please, and keep a bright lookout. It's trying on a man, I know. It would be pleasanter to come to blows. But there's no help for it till we know our men. Lay to, and whistle for a wind, that's my view."

"Jim here," said the doctor, "can help us more than anyone. The men are not shy with him, and Jim is a noticing lad."

"Hawkins, I put prodigious faith in you," added the squire.

I began to feel pretty desperate at this, for I felt altogether helpless; and yet, by an odd train of circumstances, it was indeed through me that safety came. In the meantime, talk as we pleased, there were only seven out of the twenty-six on whom we knew we could rely; and out of these seven one was a boy, so that the grown men on our side were six to their nineteen.

Introduction

*The young Geat, Beowulf, hears from a sea captain
the story of Grendel the Night Stalker, Grendel the
Man-Wolf, the Death-Shadow, and how he is
terrorizing the Danish King Hrothgar's court. Thirty
of his thanes have been slaughtered in one night.
Beowulf knows he must go immediately to Hrothgar's
aid, because Hrothgar had given shelter and help to
his father and mother in their time of need. Hrothgar,
with the wisdom of age, knows only too well how
terrible this Grendel is, and how impossible
Beowulf's task is. But Beowulf has the strength
and courage of youth. . . .*

DRAGON SLAYER

ROSEMARY SUTCLIFF

But now the shadows were gathering in the corners of the hall, and as the daylight faded, a shadow seemed to gather on the hearts of all men there, a shadow that was all too long familiar to the Danes. Then Hrothgar rose in his High Seat, and called Beowulf to him again.

"Soon it will be dusk," he said, when the young Geat stood before him. "And yet again the time of dread comes upon Heorot. You are still determined upon this desperate venture?"

"I am not wont to change my purpose without cause," Beowulf said, "and those with me are of a like mind, or they would not have taken ship with me from Geatland in the first place."

"So. Keep watch, then. If you prevail in the combat before you, you shall have such reward from me as never yet heroes had from a King. I pray to the All-Father that when the light grows again out of tonight's dark, you may stand here to claim it. Heorot is yours until morning." And he turned and walked out through the postern door, a tall old man stooping under the burden of his own height, to his sleeping quarters, where Wealhtheow the Queen had gone before him.

All up and down the hall men were taking leave of each other, dwindling away to their own sleeping places for the night. The thralls set back the benches and stacked the trestle boards against the gable-walls, and spread out straw-filled bolsters and warm wolfskin rugs for the fifteen warriors. Then they too were gone, and Heorot was left to the band of Geats, and the dreadful thing whose shadow was already creeping towards them through the dark.

"Bar the doors," Beowulf said, when the last footsteps of the last thrall had died away. "Bars will not keep him out, but at least they may give us some warning of his coming."

And when two of them had done his bidding, and the seldom-used bars were in their sockets, there was nothing more that could be done.

For a little, as the last fire sank lower, they stood about it, sometimes looking at each other, sometimes into the glowing embers, seldom speaking. Not one of them had much hope that he would see the daylight again, yet none repented of having followed their leader upon the venture. One by one, the fourteen lay down in their harness, with their swords beside them. But Beowulf stripped off his battle-sark and gave it with his sword and boar-crested helmet to Waegmund his kinsman and the dearest to him of all his companions, for he knew that mortal weapons were of no use against the Troll-kind; such creatures must be mastered, if they could be mastered at all, by a man's naked strength, and the red courage of his heart.

Then he too lay down, as though to sleep.

In the darkest hour of the spring night Grendel came
to Heorot as he had come so many times before,
up from his lair and over the high moors, through
the mists that seemed to travel with him under
the pale moon; Grendel, the Night-Stalker, the
Death-Shadow. He came to the foreporch and
snuffed about it, and smelled the man-smell,
and found that the door which had stood
unlatched for him so long was barred
and bolted. Snarling in rage that
any man should dare attempt
to keep him out, he set the
flat of his talon-tipped
hands against
the timbers
and burst
them in.

Dark as it was, the hall seemed to fill with a monstrous shadow at his coming; a shadow in which Beowulf, half springing up, then holding himself in frozen stillness, could make out no shape nor clear outline save two eyes filled with a wavering greenish flame.

The ghastly corpse-light of his own eyes showed Grendel the shapes of men as it seemed sleeping, and he did not notice among them one who leaned up on his elbow. Laughing in his throat, he reached out and grabbed young Hondscio who lay nearest to him, and almost before his victim had time to cry out, tore him limb from limb and drank the warm blood. Then, while the young warrior's dying shriek still hung upon the air, he reached for another. But this time his hand was met and seized in a grasp such as he had never felt before; a grasp that had in it the strength of thirty men. And for the first time he who had brought fear to so many caught the taste of it himself, knowing that at last he had met his match and maybe his master.

Beowulf leapt from the sleeping bench and grappled him in the darkness; and terror broke over Grendel in full force, the terror of a wild animal trapped; so that he thought no more of his hunting but only of breaking the terrible hold upon his arm and flying back into the night and the wilderness, and he howled and bellowed as he struggled for his freedom. Beowulf set his teeth and summoned all his strength and tightened his grip until the sinews cracked; and locked together they reeled and staggered up and down the great hall. Trestles and sleeping benches went over with crash on crash as they strained this way and that, trampling even through the last red embers of the dying fire; and the very walls seemed to groan and shudder as though the stout timbers would burst apart. And all the while Grendel snarled and shrieked and Beowulf fought in silence save for his gasping breaths.

Outside, the Danes listened in horror to the turmoil that seemed as though it must split Heorot asunder; and within, the Geats had sprung from their sleeping benches sword in hand, forgetful of their powerlessness against the Troll-kind, but in the dark, lit only by stray gleams of bale-fire from the monster's eyes, they dared not strike for fear of slaying their leader, and when one or other of them did contrive to get in a blow, the sword blade glanced off Grendel's charmed hide as though he were sheathed in dragon scales.

At last, when the hall was wrecked to the walls, the Night-Stalker gathered himself for one last despairing effort to break free. Beowulf's hold was as fierce as ever; yet none the less the two figures burst apart—and Grendel with a frightful shriek staggered to the doorway and through it, and fled wailing into the night, leaving his arm and shoulder torn from the roots in the hero's still unbroken grasp.

Beowulf sank down sobbing for breath on a shattered bench, and his fellows came crowding round him with torches rekindled at the scattered embers of the fire; and together they looked at the thing he held across his knees. "Not even the Troll-kind could live half a day with a wound such as that upon them," one of them said; and Waegmund agreed. "He is surely dead as though he lay here among the benches."

"Hondscio is avenged, at all events," said Beowulf. "Let us hang up this thing for a trophy, and a proof that we do not boast idly as the wind blows over."

So in triumph they nailed up the huge scaly arm on one of the roof beams above the High Seat of Hrothgar.

The first thin light of day was already washing over the moors, and almost before the grizzly thing was securely in place the Danes returned to Heorot. They came thronging in to beat

Beowulf in joyful acclaim upon his bruised and claw-marked shoulders, and gaze up in awe at the huge arm whose taloned fingers seemed even now to be striving to claw down the roof beam. Many of them called for their horses and followed the blood trail that Grendel had left in his flight up through the tilled land and over the moors until they came to the deep sea-inlet where the monster had his lair, and saw the churning waves between the rocks all fouled and boiling with blood. Meanwhile others set all things on foot for a day of rejoicing, and the young men wrestled together and raced their horses against each other, filling the day with their merrymaking, while the King's harper walked to and fro by himself under the apple trees, making a song in praise of Beowulf ready for the evening's feasting which this night would not end when darkness fell.

Introduction

It wasn't so long ago that "foundlings" (orphans with no family or home) were picked up like stray dogs and taken to the workhouse. Here life was hard and usually short. It is in the workhouse that young Oliver finds himself at the beginning of Oliver Twist. *How he copes with it, you will see. And when you read the whole book, you will discover how Oliver manages to survive despite all the sadness and cruelty and wickedness of the world around him. He's a real hero of our time, because although we no longer have workhouses today, Oliver is a reminder that many children suffer great unhappiness, and great unkindness—and survive.*

OLIVER TWIST

CHARLES DICKENS

Oliver had not been within the walls of the workhouse a quarter of an hour, and had scarcely completed the demolition of a second slice of bread, when Mr. Bumble, who had handed him over to the care of an old woman, returned; and, telling him it was a board night, informed him that the board had said he was to appear before it forthwith.

Not having a very clearly defined notion of what a live board was, Oliver was rather astounded by this intelligence, and was not quite certain whether he ought to laugh or cry. He had no time to think about the matter, however; for Mr. Bumble gave him a tap on the head, with his cane, to wake him up: and another on the back to make him lively: and bidding him follow, conducted him into a

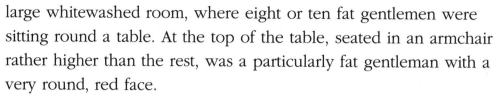

large whitewashed room, where eight or ten fat gentlemen were sitting round a table. At the top of the table, seated in an armchair rather higher than the rest, was a particularly fat gentleman with a very round, red face.

"Bow to the board," said Bumble. Oliver brushed away two or three tears that were lingering in his eyes; and seeing no board but the table, fortunately bowed to that.

"What's your name, boy?" said the gentleman in the high chair.

Oliver was frightened at the sight of so many gentlemen, which made him tremble: and the beadle gave him another tap behind, which made him cry. These two causes made him answer in a very low and hesitating voice; whereupon a gentleman in a white waistcoat said he was a fool. Which was a capital way of raising his spirits, and putting him quite at his ease.

"Boy," said the gentleman in the high chair, "listen to me. You know you're an orphan, I suppose?"

"What's that, sir?" inquired poor Oliver.

"The boy *is* a fool—I thought he was," said the gentleman in the white waistcoat.

"Hush!" said the gentleman who had spoken first. "You know you've got no father or mother, and that you were brought up by the parish, don't you?"

"Yes, sir," replied Oliver, weeping bitterly.

"What are you crying for?" inquired the gentleman in the white waistcoat. And to be sure it was very extraordinary. What *could* the boy be crying for?

"I hope you say your prayers every night," said another gentleman in a gruff voice; "and pray for the people who feed you, and take care of you—like a Christian."

"Yes, sir," stammered the boy. The gentleman who spoke last

was unconsciously right. It would have been *very* like a Christian, and a marvellously good Christian, too, if Oliver had prayed for the people who fed and took care of *him*. But he hadn't, because nobody had taught him.

"Well! You have come here to be educated, and taught a useful trade," said the red-faced gentleman in the high chair.

"So you'll begin to pick oakum to-morrow morning at six o'clock," added the surly one in the white waistcoat.

For the combination of both these blessings in the one simple process of picking oakum, Oliver bowed low by the direction of the beadle, and was then hurried away to a large ward: where, on a rough, hard bed, he sobbed himself to sleep. What a noble illustration of the tender laws of England! They let the paupers go to sleep!

Poor Oliver! He little thought, as he lay sleeping in happy unconsciousness of all around him, that the board had that very day arrived at a decision which would exercise the most material influence over all his future fortunes. But they had. And this was it:

The members of this board were very sage, deep, philosophical men; and when they came to turn their attention to the workhouse, they found out at once, what ordinary folks would never have discovered—the poor people liked it! It was a regular place of public entertainment for the poorer classes; a tavern where there was nothing to pay; a public breakfast, dinner, tea, and supper all the year round; a brick and mortar elysium, where it was all play and no work. "Oho!" said the board, looking very knowing; "we are the fellows to set this to rights; we'll stop it all, in no time." So, they established the rule, that all poor people should have the alternative (for they would compel nobody, not they), of being starved by a gradual process in the house, or by a quick one out of it. With this view, they contracted with the water-works to lay on an unlimited supply of water; and with a corn-factor to supply periodically small quantities of oatmeal; and issued three meals of thin gruel a day, with an onion twice a week, and half a roll on Sundays. They made a great many other wise and humane regulations, having reference to the ladies, which it is not necessary to repeat; kindly undertook to divorce poor married people, in consequence of the great expense of a suit in Doctors' Commons; and, instead of compelling a man to support his family, as they had theretofore done, took his family away from him, and made him a bachelor! There is no saying how many applicants for relief, under these last two heads, might have started up in all classes of society, if it had not been coupled with the workhouse; but the board were long-headed men, and had provided for this difficulty. The relief was inseparable from the workhouse and the gruel; and that frightened people.

For the first six months after Oliver Twist was removed, the system was in full operation. It was rather expensive at first, in consequence of the increase in the undertaker's bill, and the necessity of taking in the clothes of all the paupers, which fluttered loosely on their wasted, shrunken forms, after a week or two's gruel. But the number of workhouse inmates got thin as well as the paupers; and the board were in ecstasies.

The room in which the boys were fed, was a large stone hall, with a copper at one end: out of which the master, dressed in an apron for the purpose, and assisted by one or two women, ladled the gruel at meal-times. Of this festive composition each boy had one porringer, and no more—except on occasions of great public rejoicing, when he had two ounces and a quarter of bread besides. The bowls never wanted washing. The boys polished them with their spoons till they shone again; and when they had performed this operation (which never took very long, the spoons being

nearly as large as the bowls), they would sit staring at the copper, with such eager eyes, as if they could have devoured the very bricks of which it was composed; employing themselves, meanwhile, in sucking their fingers most assiduously, with the view of catching up any stray splashes of gruel that might have been cast thereon. Boys have generally excellent appetites. Oliver Twist and his companions suffered the tortures of slow starvation for three months: at last they got so voracious and wild with hunger, that one boy, who was tall for his age, and hadn't been used to that sort of thing (for his father had kept a small cook-shop), hinted darkly to his companions, that unless he had another basin of gruel *per diem*, he was afraid he might some night happen to eat the boy who slept next him, who happened to be a weakly youth of tender age. He had a wild, hungry eye; and they implicitly believed him. A council was held; lots were cast who should walk up to the master after supper that evening, and ask for more; and it fell to Oliver Twist.

The evening arrived; the boys took their places. The master, in his cook's uniform, stationed himself at the copper; his pauper assistants ranged themselves behind him; the gruel was served out; and a long grace was said over the short commons. The gruel disappeared; the boys whispered to each other, and winked at Oliver; while his next neighbours nudged him. Child as he was, he was desperate with hunger, and reckless with misery. He rose from the table; and advancing to the master, basin and spoon in hand, said: somewhat alarmed at his own temerity:

"Please, sir, I want some more."

The master was a fat, healthy man; but he turned very pale. He gazed in stupefied astonishment on the small rebel for some seconds, and then clung for support to the copper. The assistants were paralysed with wonder; the boys with fear.

"What!" said the master at length, in a faint voice.

"Please, sir," replied Oliver, "I want some more."

The master aimed a blow at Oliver's head with the ladle; pinioned him in his arms; and shrieked aloud for the beadle.

The board were sitting in solemn conclave, when Mr. Bumble rushed into the room in great excitement, and addressing the gentleman in the high chair, said,

"Mr. Limbkins, I beg your pardon, sir! Oliver Twist has asked for more!"

There was a general start. Horror was depicted on every countenance.

"For *more*!" said Mr. Limbkins. "Compose yourself, Bumble, and answer me distinctly. Do I understand that he asked for more, after he had eaten the supper allotted by the dietary?"

"He did, sir," replied Bumble.

"That boy will be hung," said the gentleman in the white waistcoat. "I know that boy will be hung."

Nobody controverted the prophetic gentleman's opinion. An animated discussion took place. Oliver was ordered into instant confinement; and a bill was next morning pasted on the outside of the gate, offering a reward of five pounds to anybody who would take Oliver Twist off the hands of the parish. In other words, five pounds and Oliver Twist were offered to any man or woman who wanted an apprentice to any trade, business, or calling.

"I never was more convinced of anything in my life," said the gentleman in the white waistcoat, as he knocked at the gate and read the bill next morning: "I never was more convinced of anything in my life, than I am that that boy will come to be hung."

Introduction

Tom Sawyer grows up in a small town on the Mississippi
River. Whether at home with his Aunt Polly or at school,
Tom's always getting himself into a pickle. In this
excerpt, he's crushed and crestfallen and feeling sorry
for himself because his girlfriend, Becky Thatcher,
whom he's done his very best to impress, won't pay
any attention to him. So Tom decides he will leave home
forever and roam abroad in the great world with his
friends, Huckleberry Finn and Joe Harper.
This is one of their marvelous capers—
my favorite one, too.

THE ADVENTURES OF TOM SAWYER

MARK TWAIN

Tom's mind was made up now. He was gloomy and desperate. He was a forsaken, friendless boy, he said; nobody loved him; when they found out what they had driven him to, perhaps they would be sorry; he had tried to do right and get along, but they would not let him; since nothing would do them but to be rid of him, let it be so; and let them blame him for the consequences —why shouldn't they? What right had the friendless to complain? Yes, they had forced him to it at last: he would lead a life of crime. There was no choice. By this time he was far down Meadow Lane, and the bell for school to "take up" tinkled faintly upon his ear. He sobbed, now, to think he should never, never hear that old familiar sound any more—it was very hard, but it was forced on him; since he was driven out into the cold world, he must submit—but he forgave them. Then the sobs came thick and fast.

Just at this point he met his soul's sworn comrade, Joe Harper—hard-eyed, and with evidently a great and dismal purpose in his heart. Plainly here were "two souls with but a single thought." Tom, wiping his eyes with his sleeve, began to blubber out something about a resolution to escape from hard usage and lack of sympathy at home by roaming abroad into the great world, never to return; and ended by hoping that Joe would not forget him.

But it transpired that this was a request which Joe had just been going to make of Tom, and had come to hunt him up for that purpose. His mother had whipped him for drinking some cream which he had never tasted and knew nothing about; it was plain that she was tired of him and wished him to go; if she felt that way, there was nothing for him to do but to succumb; he hoped she would be happy, and never regret having driven her poor boy out into the unfeeling world to suffer and die.

As the two boys walked sorrowing along, they made a new compact to stand by each other and be brothers, and never separate till death relieved them of their troubles. Then they began to lay their plans. Joe was for being a hermit, and living on crusts in a remote cave, and dying, sometime, of cold, and want, and grief; but, after listening to Tom, he conceded that there were some conspicuous advantages about a life of crime, and so he consented to be a pirate.

Three miles below St. Petersburg, at a point where the Mississippi River was a trifle over a mile wide, there was a long, narrow, wooded island, with a shallow bar at the head of it, and this offered well as a rendezvous. It was not inhabited; it lay far over towards the farther shore, abreast a dense and almost wholly unpeopled forest. So Jackson's Island was chosen.

Who were to be the subjects of their piracies was a matter that did not occur to them. Then they hunted up Huckleberry Finn, and he joined them promptly, for all careers were one to him; he was indifferent. They presently separated, to meet at a lonely spot on the river bank two miles above the village, at the favourite hour, which was midnight. There was a small log raft there which they meant to capture. Each would bring hooks and lines, and such provisions as he could steal in the most dark and mysterious way—as became outlaws; and before the afternoon was done, they had all managed to enjoy the sweet glory of spreading the fact that pretty soon the town would "hear something." All who got this vague hint were cautioned to "be mum and wait."

About midnight Tom arrived with a boiled ham and a few trifles, and stopped in a dense undergrowth on a small bluff overlooking the meeting-place. It was starlight, and very still. The mighty river lay like an ocean at rest. Tom listened a moment, but no sound disturbed the quiet. Then he gave a low, distinct whistle. It was answered from under the bluff. Tom whistled twice more; these signals were answered in the same way. Then a guarded voice said:

"Who goes there?"

"Tom Sawyer, the Black Avenger of the Spanish Main. Name your names."

"Huck Finn the Red-handed, and Joe Harper the Terror of the Seas." Tom had furnished these titles from his favourite literature.

"'Tis well. Give the countersign."

Two hoarse whispers delivered the same awful word simultaneously to the brooding night:

"BLOOD!"

Then Tom tumbled his ham over the bluff and let himself down after it, tearing both skin and clothes to some extent in the effort. There was an easy, comfortable path along the shore under the bluff, but it lacked the advantages of difficulty and danger so valued by a pirate.

The Terror of the Seas had brought a side of bacon, and had about worn himself out with getting it there. Finn the Red-handed had stolen a skillet, and a quantity of half-cured leaf-tobacco, and had also brought a few corn-cobs to make pipes with. But none of the pirates smoked or "chewed" but himself. The Black Avenger of the Spanish Main said it would never do to start without some fire. That was a wise thought; matches were hardly known there in that day. They saw a fire smouldering upon a great raft a hundred yards above, and they went stealthily thither and helped themselves to a chunk. They made an imposing adventure of it, saying "hist" every now and then and suddenly halting with finger on lip; moving with hands on imaginary dagger-hilts; and giving orders in dismal whispers that if "the foe" stirred to "let him have it to the hilt," because "dead men tell no tales." They knew well enough that the raftmen were all down at the village laying in stores or having a spree, but still that was no excuse for their conducting this thing in an unpiratical way.

They shoved off presently, Tom in command, Huck at the left oar and Joe at the forward. Tom stood amidships, gloomy-browed and with folded arms, and gave his orders in a low, stern whisper.

"Luff, and bring her to the wind!"

"Aye, aye, sir!"

"Steady, steady-y-y-y!"

"Steady it is, sir!"

"Let her go off a point!"

"Point it is, sir!"

As the boys steadily and monotonously drove the raft towards mid-stream, it was no doubt understood that these orders were given only for "style," and were not intended to mean anything in particular.

"What sail's she carrying?"

"Courses, tops'ls, and flying-jib, sir!"

"Send the r'yals up! Lay out aloft there, half a dozen of ye, foretomast-stuns'l! Lively, now!"

"Aye, aye, sir!"

"Shake out that mainto-galans'l! Sheets and braces! *Now,* my hearties!"

"Aye, aye, sir!"

"Hellum-a-lee—hard a-port! Stand by to meet her when she comes! Port, port! *Now,* men! With a will! Steady-y-y!"

"Steady it is, sir!"

The raft drew beyond the middle of the river; the boys pointed her head right and then lay on their oars. The river was not high, so there was not more than a two or three mile current.

Hardly a word was said during the next three-quarters of an hour. Now the raft was passing before the distant town. Two or three glimmering lights showed where it lay, peacefully sleeping, beyond the vague vast sweep of star-gemmed water, unconscious of the tremendous event that was happening. The Black Avenger stood still with folded arms, "looking his last" upon the scene of his former joys and his later sufferings, and wishing "she" could see him, now abroad on the wild sea, facing peril and death with dauntless heart, going to his doom with a grim smile on his lips. It was but a small strain on his imagination to remove Jackson's Island beyond eyeshot of the village, and so he "looked his last" with a broken and satisfied heart. The other pirates were looking their last, too; and they all looked so long that they came near letting the current drift them out of the range of the island. But they discovered the danger in time, and made shift to avert it. About two o'clock in the morning the raft grounded on the bar two hundred yards above the head of the island, and they waded back and forth until they had landed their freight. Part of the little raft's belongings consisted of an old sail, and this they spread over a nook in the bushes for a tent to shelter their provisions; but they themselves would sleep in the open air in good weather, as became outlaws.

They built a fire against the side of a great log twenty or thirty steps within the sombre depths of the forest, and then cooked some bacon in the frying-pan for supper, and used up half of the corn "pone" stock they had brought. It seemed glorious sport to be feasting in that wild free way in the virgin forest of an unexplored and uninhabited island, far from the haunts of men, and they said they would never return to civilization. The climbing fire lit up their faces and threw

its ruddy glare upon the pillared tree-trunks of their forest temple, and upon the varnished foliage and festooning vines. When the last crisp slice of bacon was gone, and the last allowance of corn pone devoured, the boys stretched themselves out on the grass, filled with contentment. They could have found a cooler place, but they would not deny themselves such a romantic feature as the roasting camp-fire.

"*Ain't* it jolly?" said Joe.

"It's *nuts*," said Tom.

"What would the boys say if they could see us?"

"Say? Well, they'd just die to be here—hey, Hucky?"

"I reckon so," said Huckleberry; "anyways *I'm* suited. I don't want nothing better'n this. I don't ever get enough to eat gen'ally—and here they can't come and pick at a feller and bullyrag him so."

"It's just the life for me," said Tom. "You don't have to get up, mornings, and you don't have to go to school, and wash, and all that blame foolishness."

"You see a pirate don't have to do *anything*, Joe, when he's ashore, but a hermit *he* has to be praying considerable, and then he don't have any fun, any way, all by himself that way."

"Oh yes, that's so," said Joe, "but I hadn't thought much about it, you know. I'd a good deal ruther be a pirate now that I've tried it."

"You see," said Tom, "people don't go much on hermits, now-a-days, like they used to in old times, but a pirate's always respected. And a hermit's got to sleep on the hardest place he can find, and put sackcloth and ashes on his head, and stand out in the rain, and—"

"What does he put sackcloth and ashes on his head for?" inquired Huck.

"*I* dunno. But they've *got* to do it. Hermits always do. You'd have to do that if you was a hermit."

"Dern'd if I would," said Huck.

"Well, what would you do?"

"I dunno. But I wouldn't do that."

"Why, Huck, you'd *have* to. How'd you get around it?"

"Why, I just wouldn't stand it. I'd run away."

"Run away! Well, you *would* be a nice old slouch of a hermit. You'd be a disgrace."

The Red-handed made no response, being better employed. He had finished gouging out a cob, and now he fitted a weed stem to it, loaded it with tobacco, and was pressing a coal to the charge and blowing a cloud of fragrant smoke—he was in the full bloom of luxurious contentment. The other pirates envied him this majestic vice, and secretly resolved to acquire it shortly. Presently Huck said:

"What do pirates have to do?"

Tom said:

"Oh, they have just a bully time—take ships, and burn them, and get the money and bury it in awful places in their island where there's ghosts and things to watch it, and kill everybody in the ships—make 'em walk a plank."

"And they carry the women to the island," said Joe; "they don't kill the women."

"No," assented Tom, "they don't kill the women—they're too noble. And the women's always beautiful, too."

"And don't they wear the bulliest clothes! Oh, no! All gold and silver and di'monds," said Joe with enthusiasm.

"Who?" said Huck.

"Why, the pirates."

Huck scanned his own clothing forlornly.

"I reckon I ain't dressed fit for a pirate," said he, with a regretful pathos in his voice; "but I ain't got none but these."

But the other boys told him the fine clothes would come fast enough after they should have begun their adventures. They made him understand that his poor rags would do to begin with, though it was customary for wealthy pirates to start with a proper wardrobe.

Gradually their talk died out and drowsiness began to steal upon the eyelids of the little waifs. The pipe dropped from the fingers of the Red-handed, and he slept the sleep of the conscience-free and the weary. The Terror of the Seas and the Black Avenger of the Spanish Main had more difficulty in getting to sleep. They said their prayers inwardly, and lying down, since there was nobody there with authority to make them kneel and recite aloud; in truth they had a mind not to say them at all, but they were afraid to proceed to such lengths as that, lest they might call down a sudden and special thunder-bolt from heaven. Then at once they reached and hovered upon the imminent verge of sleep—but an intruder came now that would not "down." It was conscience. They began to feel a vague fear that they had been doing wrong to run away; and next they thought of the stolen meat, and then the real torture came. They tried to argue it away by reminding conscience that they had purloined sweetmeats and apples scores of times; but conscience was not to be appeased by such thin plausibilities. It seemed to them, in the end, that there was no getting around the stubborn fact that taking sweetmeats was only "hooking" while taking bacon and ham and such valuables was plain, simple stealing—and there was a command against that in the Bible. So they inwardly resolved that so long as they remained in the business, their piracies should not again be sullied with the crime of stealing. Then conscience granted a truce, and these curiously inconsistent pirates fell peacefully to sleep.

Sir J(ames) M(atthew) Barrie (1860–1937) was born in Kirriemuir, Scotland, the ninth child in a weaver's family. As a young man he worked in London as a journalist, and he quickly became successful as a playwright and novelist. Now he is remembered best for *Peter Pan*, written first as a play in 1904 and only later (in 1911) as a story. It is dedicated to "the Five"—the orphaned sons of Sylvia Llewellyn Davies, with whom Barrie played pirates in Kensington Gardens.

Jeff Brown was born in 1926 in New York City. A magazine writer by profession, he has served on the editorial staffs of *The New Yorker, Saturday Evening Post, Life,* and *Esquire*. His series of books about Stanley Lambchop began in 1964 with the publication of *Flat Stanley*.

Carlo Collodi (1826–90) was the pseudonym of Carlo Lorenzini, who was born into a poor family in Florence, Italy. He was, in turn, a student at a seminary, a part-time soldier, a librarian, and a civil servant, until at the age of fifty he found his true vocation as a writer and translator of Perrault's fairy tales. The first story about Pinocchio appeared in a children's newspaper and was immediately popular. A collection of the stories was published in 1883 and first appeared in English translation in 1892.

Richmal Crompton (1890–1969) was the pseudonym of Richmal Crompton Lamburn, who was born in Lancashire, England. She taught at a girls' school until polio crippled her in 1923, forcing her to give up her job. She had already started to write stories about William Brown for adult readers of *Home Magazine*, and, when published in book form (more than forty in her lifetime), they became popular with children, too. It is said that William has many characteristics of her own brother.

Roald Dahl (1916–90) was born in South Wales to Norwegian parents. In his autobiography, *Boy* (1984), he describes how rather than going to college, he wanted a job that would take him to "a wonderful faraway place." After working in East Africa he became a fighter pilot during World War II, and it was while he was stationed in Washington as Assistant Air Attache that he began to write. *Charlie and the Chocolate Factory*, published in 1964, was a major success, and many more books for children followed. The illustrations of Quentin Blake (the U.K.'s first Children's Laureate) have become synonymous with Roald Dahl's stories.

Charles Dickens (1812–70) was born in Portsmouth, England. He never forgot his family's misery when his father was sent to prison for debt and, aged twelve, he went to work in a blacking factory. With great determination he became a shorthand reporter in Parliament and went on to write novels that made him immensely popular in both the U.K. and the U.S. First appearing in short parts in the monthly magazine *Bentley's Miscellany, Oliver Twist* was published in book form in 1838.

Jean Craighead George was born in 1919 in Washington, DC. She learned about living off the land when her father took her and her brothers exploring along the Potomac River. She even planned to run away from home (as Sam Gribley does), but was back within the hour! She has written many more stories about animals and nature, including *Julie of the Wolves*, which won the American Library Association Newbery Medal in 1973. *My Side of the Mountain* was published in 1959.

Ted Hughes (1930–98) was born in Yorkshire, England. After graduating from college, he worked at a number of jobs (rose gardener, night watchman, zoo attendant) until his writing brought him recognition as a poet and playwright of great power and accomplishment. In 1984 he became the U.K.'s Poet Laureate. *The Iron Man* (retitled *The Iron Giant* in the U.S.) was published in 1968 and made into an animated film in 1999.

Rudyard Kipling (1865–1936) was born in Bombay, India. Sent home to England to go to school, he was wretchedly unhappy, but returned to India in 1882 as a journalist, which was the start of his career as an author and poet. He wrote the first Mowgli story while living with his American wife in Vermont, and it was published in the children's magazine *St. Nicholas* in 1894. The six stories that make up the first *Jungle Book* appeared in book form later that year.

C(live) S(taples) Lewis (1898–1963) was born in Belfast, Northern Ireland. He had a lonely childhood and found his chief pleasure in reading. He grew up to become a scholar of English Literature, teaching at the universities of both Oxford and Cambridge. He wrote books of literary criticism and religious study, as well as science fiction novels and stories for children. *The Lion, the Witch and the Wardrobe*, published in 1950, was the first of seven *Chronicles of Narnia*, which were, he said, "the books I should have liked to read . . . that's always been my reason for writing."

A(lan) A(lexander) Milne (1882–1956) was born in London, England. He was a journalist and assistant editor of the humorous magazine *Punch* before becoming a successful playwright in the 1920s. His first book of verse for children, *When We Were Very Young*, published in 1924, sold so many copies that his publishers begged for more. *Winnie-the-Pooh* (1926) was written for and about his son, Christopher Robin, and the animals are based on the toys in his nursery. They can still be seen in the New York Public Library. "The Forest," too, is a real place: Ashdown Forest in Sussex, England, to which Milne took the artist, Ernest Shepard, when the illustrations were planned.

Michael Morpurgo was born in 1943 in St. Albans, England. Like Bertie in *The Butterfly Lion*, published in 1996, he was very homesick when sent away to boarding school. He took refuge in reading, particularly poetry, and Stevenson's *Treasure Island* became, and remains, his favorite book. He has written many books for children, including *The Wreck of the Zanzibar*, which won the Whitbread Children's Novel Award.

(Ann) Philippa Pearce was born in 1920 in Cambridgeshire, England. She grew up in the mill- house that is the setting for *Tom's Midnight Garden*, and still lives nearby. The book, published in 1958, won the Library Association Carnegie Medal. Philippa Pearce has written many other books for children, notably *A Dog So Small* and *The Way to Sattin Shore*.

Robert Louis Stevenson (1850–94) was born in Edinburgh, Scotland, and spent much of his short life traveling in search of a climate that might cure what is now thought to have been tuberculosis. In 1881, on a rainy day in Braemar, he drew a map of an imaginary island to entertain his American stepson, Lloyd Osbourne. This was the inspiration for *Treasure Island*, which appeared first as a serial called *The Sea Cook*. When published in book form in 1883, it established Stevenson as a master of the adventure story.

Rosemary Sutcliff (1920–92) was born in Surrey, England. As she tells us in her autobiography, *Blue Remembered Hills* (1983), she was a solitary child, being afflicted with Still's Disease at the age of two. This prevented her from pursuing her first love, painting (she could neither stand at an easel nor reach across a canvas), so she turned her powerful imagination to writing historical novels. It also meant that her mother taught her at home, reading legends, history, and the story of Beowulf to her—which later inspired her own retelling, published in 1961.

Mark Twain (1835–1910) was the pseudonym of Samuel Langhorne Clemens. He worked as a riverboat pilot on the Mississippi River, and used this experience when he wrote *Tom Sawyer* (1876) and, later, *Huckleberry Finn* (1884), both of which are based on his boyhood memories of Hannibal, Missouri, the town on the Mississippi River where he grew up. A successful journalist, he also wrote a number of books especially for children, including *The Prince and the Pauper*.

T(erence) H(anbury) White (1906–64) was born in Bombay, India, and brought to England when he was five. He was a teacher before becoming a full-time writer and spent his later years living in the Channel Islands. *The Sword in the Stone* was published in 1938, but twenty years later White revised it for inclusion in *The Once and Future King*, his retelling of the complete Arthurian epic. He was profoundly influenced by Sir Thomas Malory's *Morte d'Arthur*, admitting, "I have tried to look at it through the innocent eyes of young people, because I don't very much believe in the modern theory that the whole object of life is gratified desire. Malory didn't either."

ACKNOWLEDGEMENTS

The publisher would like to thank the copyright holders for permission to reproduce the following copyright material:

J. M. Barrie: Great Ormond Street Children's Hospital for "The Flight" from *Peter Pan* by J. M. Barrie, Scribner 1911. Copyright © 1911 by J. M. Barrie. **Pauline Baynes:** HarperCollins Publishers Ltd. for illustrations by Pauline Baynes from *The Lion, The Witch and the Wardrobe* by C. S. Lewis from *The Complete Chronicles of Narnia*, Collins 1998. Illustrations copyright © HarperCollins Publishers Ltd. 1950, color illustrations © HarperCollins Publishers Ltd. 1998. **Christian Birmingham:** The Artworks for illustration on p. 52 by Christian Birmingham and HarperCollins Publishers Ltd. for all other illustrations by Christian Birmingham from *The Butterfly Lion* by Michael Morpurgo, Viking 1997. Copyright © Christian Birmingham 1996. **Quentin Blake:** A. P. Watt Ltd. for illustrations by Quentin Blake from *Charlie and the Chocolate Factory* by Roald Dahl, from *The Roald Dahl Treasury*, Viking 1997. Copyright © Quentin Blake 1997. A. P. Watt Ltd. for illustration on p. 41 by Quentin Blake from *Charlie and the Chocolate Factory* by Roald Dahl, Viking 1997. Copyright © Quentin Blake 1995, 1997. **Jeff Brown:** HarperCollins Publishers Inc. for extract from *Flat Stanley*, HarperCollins 1964. Copyright © 1964, renewed 1992 by Jeff Brown. **Carlo Collodi:** Penguin Books Ltd. for extract from *Pinocchio* by Carlo Collodi translated by E. Harden, Puffin 1974, 1996. Translation copyright © The Estate of E. Harden 1974, 1996. **Richmal Crompton:** Macmillan Children's Books, London, for "The Fall of the Idol" from *Just William* by Richmal Crompton. Copyright Richmal C. Ashbee. **Roald Dahl:** Alfred A. Knopf Children's Books, a division of Random House Inc. for extract from *Charlie and the Chocolate Factory* by Roald Dahl, Alfred A. Knopf Inc. 1964. Copyright © 1964 by Roald Dahl. Copyright renewed 1992 by Felicity Dahl, Tessa Dahl, Theo Dahl, Ophelia Dahl, and Lucy Dahl Faircloth. Copyright assigned to Roald Dahl Limited 1994. **Andrew Davidson:** Alfred A. Knopf Children's Books, a division of Random House Inc. for illustrations by Andrew Davidson from *The Iron Giant* by Ted Hughes, Harper 1968. Copyright © 1985 by Faber and Faber Limited. **Jean Craighead George:** Dutton Children's Books, a division of Penguin Putnam Inc. for "In Which I Get Started on This Venture" from *My Side of the Mountain* by Jean Craighead George, E. P. Dutton 1959. Copyright © 1959, renewed 1987 by Jean Craighead George. **Ted Hughes:** Alfred A. Knopf Children's Books, a division of Random House Inc. for "The Return of the Iron Giant" from *The Iron Man* by Ted Hughes, Harper 1968. Copyright © 1968, renewed 1996 by Ted Hughes. **Rudyard Kipling:** A. P. Watt Ltd. on behalf of The National Trust for Places of Historic Interest or Natural Beauty for extract from *The Jungle Book* by Rudyard Kipling, Century 1894. **C. S. Lewis:** *The Lion, the Witch and the Wardrobe* by C. S. Lewis copyright © C. S. Pte. Ltd. 1950. Extract reprinted by permission. **A. A. Milne:** Dutton Children's Books, a division of Penguin Putnam Inc. for "In Which Pooh Goes Visiting and Gets Into a Tight Place" from *Winnie-the-Pooh* by A. A. Milne, E. P. Dutton 1926. Copyright © 1926 by E. P. Dutton, renewed 1954 by A. A. Milne. **Michael Morpurgo:** HarperCollins Publishers Ltd. for "Bertie and the Lion" from *The Butterfly Lion* by Michael Morpurgo, Viking 1997. Copyright © Michael Morpurgo 1996. **Philippa Pearce:** Oxford University Press for "Through a Door" from *Tom's Midnight Garden*, Lippincott 1958. Copyright © Oxford University Press 1958. **E. H. Shepard:** Curtis Brown Ltd., London, for line illustrations by E. H. Shepard from *Winnie-the-Pooh* by A. A. Milne. Copyright under the Berne Convention, coloring copyright © 1970, 1973 by E. H. Shepard and Methuen Children's Books. **Rosemary Sutcliff:** Dutton Children's Books, a division of Penguin Putnam Inc. for extract from *Beowulf* by Rosemary Sutcliff, E. P. Dutton 1962. Copyright © 1961, renewed 1989 by Rosemary Sutcliff. **Tomi Ungerer:** Diogenes Verlag AG, Zürich, for illustrations by Tomi Ungerer from *Flat Stanley* by Jeff Brown, Methuen & Co. Ltd. 1968. Copyright © by Diogenes Verlag AG, Zürich. **T. H. White:** David Higham Associates Limited for extract from *The Sword in the Stone* by T. H. White, Putnam 1939. Copyright © T. H. White 1938.

Every effort has been made to obtain permission to reproduce copyright material, but there may be cases where we have been unable to trace a copyright holder. The publisher will be happy to correct any omissions in future printings.

The publisher would like to thank the following artists for their original illustrations:

Ian Andrew: illustrations for *The Jungle Book* © Ian Andrew 2000. **Peter Bailey:** illustrations for *Pinocchio* © Peter Bailey 2000. **Christian Birmingham:** border illustration for *The Butterfly Lion* © Christian Birmingham 2000. **Emma Chichester Clark:** illustrations for *Peter Pan* © Emma Chichester Clark 2000. **Robin Bell Corfield:** illustrations for *The Adventures of Tom Sawyer* © Robin Bell Corfield 2000. **Chris Fisher:** illustrations for *The Sword in the Stone* © Chris Fisher 2000. **Michael Foreman:** illustrations for *Dragon Slayer* © Michael Foreman 2000. **Felicity Gill:** illustrations for *My Side of the Mountain* © Felicity Gill 2000. **Richard Jones:** illustrations for *Oliver Twist* © Richard Jones 2000. **Stephen Lambert:** illustrations for *Tom's Midnight Garden* © Stephen Lambert 2000. **John Lawrence:** illustrations for *Treasure Island* © John Lawrence 2000. **Tony Ross:** illustrations for *Just William* © Tony Ross 2000.